Ghosts of

the

Missouri River

By Marcia Schwartz

Some illustrations by
David von Behren

Table of Contents

Dedicated to the men in my life:
Hank, Lance and Reed.

The reader should understand that we were able to obtain some of these stories only if we promised to obscure the actual identity of persons and/or property. This required us to occasionally use fictitious names. In such cases, the names of the people and/or the places are not to be confused with actual places or actual persons living or dead.

Ghosts along the Missouri River?
Yep, there's lots of 'em.
There is quite a collection of folks...
robbers & school teachers, ladies of the evening and cowboys...
even most proper little old ladies and critters.

The one thing they have in common is a connection to the Big
Muddy...some even ending up under it.

The Bells Of St. DeRoin

Miss Fanny came to be our teacher at old St. DeRoin school in 1875. She crossed the Missouri River on a ferry and landed at the trading post which was called St. DeRoin.

The settlers had built a schoolhouse out of native brick and they were mighty proud of their structure. Most schoolhouses thereabouts were simple wooden buildings, but this schoolhouse out-rivaled them all. It was built at the top of the bluff, right next to the St. DeRoin cemetery. Now, most schoolhouses had a bell to call the children in to start the day and for recess. But St. DeRoin had two bells – a smaller hand-rung type and a large, tolling bell housed in a tower. The latter had been floated across the river on a barge and had been a costly investment by the farmers and traders of this thriving community. They were quite proud of this huge iron bell which could be heard for miles around.

When the president of the school board, Mr. Ackers, showed Miss Fanny the bell on the day that she applied for the job as

schoolmistress, it is reported that she was quite impressed. "May I pull the rope and try it out?" she asked.

"Well, go ahead, but don't keep at it too long or you'll have all the cattle from miles around bearing down on us. Don't want to wake the dead, either," he chuckled, pointing to the cemetery beyond the schoolyard.

Miss Fanny was hired that day. She was a spunky, redheaded, educated lady from back east somewhere.

There were twenty-two of us who clunked up the wooden steps of St. DeRoin school a few days later. Boys clad in overalls, girls in calico dresses, all of us carrying tin pails containing our lunches. We bounded into the entry hall where a smiling Miss Fanny still held the thick rope of the bell she had been ringing.

"Good morning, Miss Fanny!" we trilled as we dropped our pails and hung caps and scarves on wooden pegs of the entry before assembling inside the main schoolroom. We waited to be assigned to desks with inkwells and initials pencil-carved into the wooden tops by former students.

We were arranged by size, the smaller children in smaller desks on the right, the larger children proceeding to the left. We eagerly vied for the tasks of hanging out the flag and bringing in a bucket of water from the pump outside. As the days became cooler, there would be logs brought in by the bigger boys to feed the pot-bellied stove. But on this lovely late summer day, there was no need of that. We soon learned that our young, smiley schoolmarm could also be demanding.

"Don't go out of the schoolyard at recess. There are rattlesnakes in the bluffs hereabouts," she warned. "And don't ever go into the cemetery. It isn't polite to step on the graves of the dead!"

We began to wonder if it was just "politeness" Miss Fanny was concerned about. Little by little, we learned that she was afraid of many things – spiders, snakes, buzzards – and most of all, she was afraid of the spirits that hovered about a cemetery. Josiah, an eighth grader, asked to go to the outhouse on a dark gloomy day just before Halloween. While he was out there, he hung a sheet he had brought from home over a brambleberry bush growing in the fence between the schoolhouse yard and

the cemetery. Then he set up a howling like a wounded coon dog. Miss Fanny flew to the window and became quite panicked. Before we knew it, she was out in the entry pulling on the bell tower rope as hard and fast as she could. We all giggled and called her "scaredy cat," behind her back, of course.

Mr. Ackers, who lived nearby, soon came into the schoolhouse and handed Miss Fanny the sheet. Miss Fanny smiled sheepishly. "I'm sorry to have bothered you, Mr. Ackers." She turned to her desk, sat down and pretended to be writing in a notebook until it was 4 o'clock and time for dismissal.

She never scolded or chided Josiah or any of us, and it looked like there were tears in her eyes when she bid us goodbye at the schoolhouse door. As we tripped down the bluff toward town, we told Josiah he should apologize. I don't know if he ever did, and I never heard any more about the incident.

After that, things calmed down and we all tried to please Miss Fanny more than ever. One day in November we had a visitor. Mr. Haggai Craterman came calling. Now, all of our families knew old Haggai. He was a "river rat," a rough and bearded codger who worked loading and unloading the river barges. Usually he worked down near St. Joseph, but on this particular day, he had come up river to help the farmers load their hogs on a barge. He was a heavily bearded, spitting, cussing man. Our parents had told us, "Just stay out of his way, and pay him no mind. He hasn't hurt anyone yet, but don't go riling him up."

Haggai stood about 6'7", a whale of a man who could pick a 300-pound hog above his head and toss it, oinking and squealing, onto a barge. We children liked to hide in the trees and watch him toss those big sows through the air like they were acorns.

As I said, Haggai came to school one day. He was at the pump scooping water into his hands for a drink when we were coming out for recess.

Miss Fanny called me aside, "Hsst, Tom, who is that man at the well?"

"That's old Haggai, the hog man," I explained. "Pay him no mind."

But Miss Fanny, she wasn't about to let that varmint hang around her schoolyard. She rang the hand bell. "Go inside, children!"

"But recess just started!" Josiah whined.

"GO, NOW!" she pointed to the door. We peeked from the half-open door to see her approach Haggai, "Please go away. Get your drink somewhere else," she said in her demanding voice.

"I ain't hurting nothin'! Who do you think you are, tellin' me what to do?"

"I am Miss Fanny, and if you don't leave immediately, I will call for help."

Haggai backed away, spitting water from his mouth and wiping his beard. He crawled through the fence and entered the cemetery. Miss Fanny came back inside. We resumed 'rithmetic class, though we could see that she was red-faced and flustered.

It wasn't ten minutes later and old Haggai strode through the door and walked menacingly toward Miss Fanny who stood near her desk at the rear of the room. There was no way she could run to the bell tower rope, so she picked up the small hand bell and raised it over her head.

"GET OUT OF HERE!" she screamed at Haggai.

"Ain't no #?@&* schoolteacher hussy gonna tell me where to go!" He stood there spitting tobacco juice on the wooden floor.

"Run, children, run as fast as you can and get help!" Frozen in horror and then, within seconds, following Josiah's lead, we leapt from our desks and headed for the door, spilling out in various directions as we ran for help. Breathless, we entered our homes or crawled across fences to the fields, calling to our fathers to come to Miss Fanny's aid. But before any of us reached our destinations, we heard the huge bell in the tower, pealing and donging frantically.

My dad and Mr. Ackers were the first men to get to the schoolhouse after we roused them. There on the entry floor they found old Haggai, blood flowing from a gash on his head. The hand bell was lying nearby. Old Haggai was dead. No one seemed to be aware of any next of kin, so some of the men buried him up in a far corner of the cemetery.

We never did see Miss Fanny again. How she so quickly vanished from the scene remains a mystery. Did she take off through that dreaded cemetery and somehow disappear into the thick timber on the other side? We'll probably never know what became of her.

But this one thing we do know, even though the schoolhouse has been abandoned after these many years and our children are now bussed to neighboring towns, on many dark nights, the bell in the old schoolhouse tower dongs loudly. Some say they can also hear the reply of the smaller schoolmarm bell. We wonder, could it be the ghost of Haggai ringing those bells, or could it be Miss Fanny herself!

The Ghost Rider Of The Pony Express

Billy Edwards leaped through the door of his family's farmhouse on that fateful day in March 1860. He had just ridden his pony home on the Kansas side from the ferry which crossed the Missouri River to St. Joseph. He threw a satchel of supplies he had purchased for his mother on the kitchen table and pulled out a parchment flyer.

"Look, Ma, they're advertisin' for Pony Express riders. They want a guy just like me to carry the mail twenty miles from station to station on the relay that will reach to San Francisco, California. This is the chance of a lifetime!"

Billy's mother, Marie Edwards, had heard about this remarkable plan – who hadn't in these parts? She sighed, wiped her hands on her apron and took the flyer from his hand. Scanning it quickly, she gasped as she read, "Wanted. Wiry young men, preferably orphans, to ride 20 miles… PREFERABLY ORPHANS! You are not an orphan, Billy."

"Well, I'm wiry and light in the saddle. You know I win just about every pony race around!"

"Probably they want orphans because this is such a foolhardy, dangerous plan!"

"But, Ma, I've just got to do this – I could make good money for our family."

Marie resumed wringing out the clothes in a large tub. "Take it up with your father when he comes in from milking, but I know what his answer will be. He needs you here to help with the farm work!"

"Ah, drat! Farm work! Farm work! Farm work! That's all I ever hear. I want to get out in the world and do something brave and exciting!" Billy stomped off to stable his pony.

Later, Pa Edwards agreed with his wife. Billy was too young! He was needed at home! The Pony Express business was too dangerous. "The prairie is full of gopher holes and sage. There will be bad weather, rough trails, Indians and wild animals to contend with. No, son, you stay right here. Your Ma and I have already lost three children to the fever. It would kill your ma if she lost you, too."

Billy pouted and said no more. But the romantic lure of being a heroic Pony Express Rider danced in his head both day and night, and on his next trip from their Wathena farm, he again crossed on the ferry to St. Joseph, and inquired further. Indeed, Russell, Majors and Waddell, the fathers of this grand scheme, were still advertising for riders for the four hundred superior horses which they had purchased for the high price of about two hundred dollars a head.

At the Pony Express stable on Penn Street, Billy admired the fine bay mare that would carry the first rider, a Johnny Frye, on the first leg of the journey to Marysville, Kansas, which, if everything went according to plan, should be accomplished in 12 hours. The next leg would be to Fort Kearney in Nebraska in, hopefully, 34 hours. The riders would be supplied with fresh mounts every 10 miles or so. Billy learned that the cost to post a piece of mail was $6.90 for the first 10 words, and 10 cents a word after that.

The couriers were advised to ride with a minimum of gear, though a rifle could rightfully be included. No excess weight could be tolerated if these horses were going to run from ten to twenty-five miles per hour.

On this fresh spring morning of April 3, 1860, the bay mare had to be kept in the stable before departing because the excited crowds were plucking hairs from her mane and tail for souvenirs.

Billy looked on amid all the activity; even fellas in high office like the mayor were there. The mayor gave a fancy little talk and personally handed the pouch of mail up to Johnny Frye.

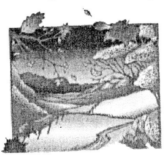

The bay clattered down the cobblestone street to the ferry. When they landed on the other side, Johnny urged the mare up the Kansas embankment where more crowds hallooed him as he thundered off across the prairie.

Billy returned home that evening with the Pony Express oath in his pocket. He read it again by the candlelight in his room. "I, _____, swear," it began. "Ma ought to read the oath which vowed not to use profane language, not to drink intoxicating liquors, not to fight or quarrel with other employees of the Pony Express, and to conduct 'honestly and with faithfulness my duties. So help me God!'" Billy signed his name to the oath and sneaked back to St. Joseph a few days later.

He left a short note on the kitchen table, apologizing to his ma and pa. "I'm sorry to disobey you, but this is something I just have to do, or die. You've done a good job of rearing me, and I will be all right. I want to make you both proud of me. Love, Billy."

A few months later, a representative from the Pony Express appeared at the door of the Edwards' farmhouse. His news wasn't good. There had been an uprising of the Paiute Indians and he was sorry to inform them that Billy had been killed as he rode through their lands.

Ma was heartbroken. Even Billy's daring and bravery couldn't ease the sadness that engulfed her. Maybe it was a gift that she claimed she could hear Billy thundering past their farmhouse on the south forty many nights as she lay restless and crying. "It was Billy, I know it was!" she exclaimed to Pa who just shook his head.

The Pony Express was only in operation for 18 months until the completion of the transcontinental telegraph made the business obsolete. But in that short time, 308 runs had been made both ways from Missouri to California, an amazing feat, but not a paying one as Russell, Majors and Waddell lost their shirts.

Billy was buried close to the place where he had fallen and was honored all along the trail as word spread of his daring and sacrifice. And, of course, Ma and Pa have long ago also passed over to the other side.

The strange thing is this: the families who have lived near the south forty sometimes still hear the echo of a fast horse's hooves pounding the earth, especially on a night when the air is light and clear.

Rescue On The Bridge

The lights of the oncoming car caused Christine to squint as she approached the tollbooth on foot. She handed the operator a quarter from her precious pocket of tips, the cost for a pedestrian to cross the Missouri River bridge. Her old Studebaker car had conked out on the other side of the bridge as she was coming to her waitress job at the Last Chance Café on the Nebraska side of the river that morning.

To get to work on time, Christine had just abandoned her car and walked across the bridge. Maybe it would start now. If not, she'd have to walk or hitchhike to Fortesque, Missouri, where she lived.

After a long day of serving catfish or carp meals in the riverbank café, she was weary and smelly from the fumes of deep-fat fried fish and chips. She had been on her feet all day. Her back was tired and her feet ached. But worse than any bodily discomfort was the emotional pain of depression which enshrouded her.

The neon lights of the café
sign glowed below her as
she trudged up the rise in the
bridge span. She was so tired
– so tired of working this job
and still barely getting ahead.
It was 1945, the country
was recovering from the
World War and the collapse
of the economy in the '30s,
but Christine's world was
shrinking, caving in upon
her. She had two small
children to support since her
errant, alcoholic husband
had deserted her. One night
he pulled the car to the side of the road and jumped out of the
Studebaker in the midst of a quarrel as they drove home from
Omaha after visiting her parents.

Christine, Tommy and Susan had waited there until almost
morning and when it seemed, at last, that Lester would not
return, she moved behind the wheel and shakily followed the
road toward home. She was not an experienced driver, but
somehow she made it. They waited for days. The children cried
for their father; she cried, too. He hadn't been a very good
husband or father, but better than no support at all. Though they
waited for months, Lester never came home. It was as if he had
walked into the dark night and fallen off the face of the earth.

That was two years ago. Christine had found the job of being
a waitress and called upon a kindly, grandmotherly neighbor
in Fortesque to watch her children so she could pay a small
babysitting fee, pay the rent, buy gas for the car and eat!

Her parents in Omaha would probably have helped her, but she was too proud to go to them to tell about the desertion of a husband that they had begged her not to marry. "He's too old for you! He's an itinerant worker with a questionable past! He's too old for you! He drinks too much! He'll break your heart!" But Christine had not heeded their warnings. She had stormed out of the house and eloped with Lester.

She had seen her mother and father only a few times since that day. There was little communication between them. And in the few visits to her former home, there was barely a polite tolerance on all sides. Perhaps that tenseness contributed to the final quarrel between the young couple and led to Lester's escape.

As Christine reached the crest of the bridge, tears had started flooding her cheeks. She looked down into the swirling dark eddies of the river below her. She saw pieces of driftwood, loosened from the banks by an earlier storm, as they tossed and bobbed upon the currents. And suddenly, Christine felt an overwhelming urge to pull herself up on the railing and drop into the dark depths of the river! Maybe in death she could find freedom from this spiritual pain that was pulling her down and down into the dark, swirling depths in her own soul.

Christine grabbed a girder, hoisted herself up on the narrow railing. Her children would be better off with the kindly neighbor than with her. She hesitated momentarily – and then in a dousing of reality – What on earth was the matter with her! Coming out of a fog she realized, "I need to get down from here before I fall!" Just then one foot slipped from the wet

surface of the railing and she nearly fell into the churning hell below her, but she felt a man's strong hand grab her arm and steady her.

"Hold on, Christine, I'll help you get back to this side." She looked into the handsome face of a stranger. She noticed a plaid flannel shirt and shoulder-length blond hair.

Once to safety, she collapsed against his chest, crying. "Thank you," she gasped when she could finally speak. Seeing how shaken she was, the stranger lifted her in his arms and carried her down the Missouri approach to her car. He opened the door and gently deposited her behind the wheel of the Studebaker.

"My car won't run," she blurted out.

"I know. Let me take a look at it," he said in a very reassuring tone. He unlatched the hood and jiggled some wires. "Turn the ignition," he said. Christine did as he said and the engine immediately cranked over and started.

The stranger came to her door and patted her shoulder. "Christine," he said, "I know you are going through a rough patch, but don't give up. Things will get better. Go to Omaha and make up with your parents. They love you and the children. Give them a chance, and give life a chance...OK?" He smiled with a glowing warmth that she had never before seen in a man.

"Thank you," she breathed. "Thank you..." she hesitated, wanting to say a name she did not know.

"Luke. Luke O'Bryan," he offered.

"Thank you, Luke. I'm so glad you were on the bridge tonight and rescued me. Thank you SO much!"

"It was my pleasure, Christine." As she pulled the car into a wide circle across the roadway to head back east, she glanced in her rearview mirror for one last glance at the remarkable stranger, but there was no one there. How did he know her name and circumstances? She couldn't remember him ever coming into the café.

However, she did do as he said. She went to her parents who gladly took in Christine and the children. She enrolled in a secretarial school, and the children thrived in their new environment, living with adoring grandparents.

Throughout the next several years, Christine thought often of the man who had done so much for her that dark night on the bridge, and she determined to go to Rulo and look up Luke O'Bryan. He had been right about everything, and she wanted to thank him with all her heart for she was happier than she ever thought she could be on that unforgettable night on the bridge.

So one fall day, Christine returned to the café. Some of the old regulars were there, playing cards at a corner table. After the "howdy-dos" all around, Christine asked if any of them knew a Luke O'Bryan. "He saved my life once and I want to thank him!"

"Can't say as I do," said Willy Ivers. But after a while, Jim Sterling rubbed his scratchy beard and said, "You know, I think that was the name of the fella that was working on the construction gang that built the bridge. He fell off a high girder to his death. That was in '38 or '39, I believe. Yep! His name was Luke O'Bryan…a good-lookin' young blond fella!"

Skeleton Pulls Corpse From River

South Sioux City Herald, November 12, 1992

A phantom appeared before the eyes of Amy Lawson as she was jogging on a path near the Missouri River last night. She described a large skeleton which glowed eerily in the moonlight. It was tugging something from the freezing water that appeared to be a huge corpse. When it noticed Amy on the path above it, it faded away, as did the bulky thing it wrestled.

This is not the first time that a phantom-being has been sighted along the riverbank. Residents are cautioned to stay way from the area for the ghost appears to be quite strong and could be dangerous.

The ghost speaks:

Ah, I'm not that dangerous – I just want to be left alone. I ain't kilt anything but grizzly bears, buffalo and Indians all me life, and that was over a hundred years ago. Well, I guess that don't count all the beaver I caught fer their pelts.

You see, I'm Hugh Glass, one of the most famous fur traders ever, even if I do say so meself. I'm the one that survived a grizzly bear maulin' that would have kilt mos' men.

It all began in 1823 when General William Ashley invited me to join a trading party for the Rocky Mountain Fur Company. They had recently obtained a license to trade on the upper Missouri River.

I was huntin' all alone one day that summer in what is now South Dakota when I surprised a female grizzly and her cubs in a thicket. Now anyone who knows anything about animals west of the Mississippi knows that there's nothin' fiercer under God's sun than a mother grizzly who's protectin' her young 'uns.

That crazed bear lunged at me an' my horse. Before I could fire my rifle, she had thrown me on the ground, growlin' like a maniac. I drew my knife, which was barely longer than the bear's claws, and stabbed and stabbed at her as she kept rakin' me with her claws an' throwin' me around.

My comrades found me, a sorry-lookin' mound of bloody flesh, the next day. Some accounts say a dead bear lay nearby, but I'll tell ye the bloody truth, she hobbled away jes' as I was passin' out. Well, when my party found me the next day, I was so broken and gashed open, they didn't figger I could last through the night.

They needed to be movin' eastward so they dug a shallow grave and left the 17-year-old Jim Bridger and John Fitzgerald to bury me once I heaved me last.

Those two say they waited six days, watchin' my struggling chest rise and fall. They also say the reason they lit out on their horses was because they heard the Arikara warriors nearby. But what in tarnation made them take my tools of survival with them in their flight!

The next mornin' I became conscious again and crawled to the Grand River there by the campsite. The river reflected back the most God-awful sight – my bloodied, mangled face! And I became enraged when I realized my so-called friends had deserted me in the wilderness without a horse, food, gin, gun or knife!

I was so dag-blasted, hell-fire mad at those coots that I determined that I would stay alive an' I would kill 'em when I found 'em. I had me a broken leg, so I jes' crawled through the wilderness, eating roots, berries, bugs, anything jes' to stay alive. As I crawled along, I was burnin' with fever and I was burnin' with rage, an' that kept me fueled to just keep goin' on.

I traveled at night to get away from the Indians and the heat of the sun. Once I found an abandoned campsite with a pack of wild dogs circlin' nearby. Something gleamed from the ashes – an old buck knife. Laying real still until one of them dogs came up to sniff me, I was able to git one 'round the neck and stab 'im. I feasted on raw meat for several days and then continued my quest for revenge.

It took me several weeks crawlin' an' hobblin' more than 100 miles until I reached the Missouri River. With the help of the old buck knife, I built me a floater and drifted another 100 miles down to Fort Kiowa where my fur party was headquartered.

Thus, I completed a miraculous 200-mile trek, accomplished by a man in the most pitiable of conditions. My story has been celebrated in a novel, "Lord Grizzly" by Fredrick Manfred, and "The Song of Hugh Glass" by Nebraska poet laureate John Niehardt, as well as many other books and movies.

But, here's the funny part: when I finally came face to face with Bridger and Fitzgerald, I couldn't kill 'em. I learned me somethin' – a man's gotta forgive or that anger is jes' gonna eat 'em up – so I forgave 'em.

History writes that I was killed, along with two fellow trappers, ten years later by Arikara Indians in an attack on the Yellowstone River. It didn't happen there. Actually, in my travels, I ran into that ol' grizzly bear that I had fought earlier. I recognized her from the ear that I bit off in our fight. This las' time I met up with her, we were high on a bluff above the Missouri River south of Yankton. We looked each other in the eye, an' we jes' commenced to lay into each other again, since the outcome of a winner in the former tussle was still in doubt.

We got ourselves wrapped up in one big ball, and we plummeted straight down into the depths of the Missouri.

The undercurrent pulled us along 'til we were beached down aroun' South Sioux City. After all these years, we are jes' about in a dead heat. She won't give up, and I'm a stubborn cuss an' I won't give in!

That's why my bony ol' body keeps a pullin' her ashore, an' she keeps rollin' back in the water, tryin' to pull me in with her. That's not a human corpse I'm tryin' to pull out of the river, it's that cranky ol' bear carcass, and I reckon you'll see us still rasslin' there along the banks of the Missouri River for another century or so, for neither one of us is about to give up!

The Ghost Of Main Street

Charles Rouleau, a Frenchman, married a half-breed woman which entitled them to land on the Half-Breed tract in southeast Nebraska. He founded a town on the Missouri River bank in 1855 which was an ideal location situated on the bluffs above a great bend in the river where the eye can survey the graceful curves of the river and gaze across the bottom ground of Missouri on the other side. It was prime for trade and travel and became a hub of the westward movement. The town was called Rouleau, but somehow became shortened to Rulo.

Charles could have become a very wealthy man, but he had a tendency to be too generous. He sold plots in Rulo for very modest prices, or gave them away.

There was a perfect storm of building as fishermen, farmers, tradesmen and merchants contributed to the boom of Rulo. As could be expected, banks emerged to manage a growing financial world – at one time there were three banks along First Street. Thirty-one businesses lined the streets of this thriving

town. And even though Rouleau wasn't exactly a rich man, he was comfortable in a stately brick home on one of the steep hills that backed the main street, a good distance from the fishy-smelling riverfront.

Rouleau took pride in this bustling place. He was a kindly old city father, well liked by the citizenry.

Rulo had been a rather lawless town in the beginning but now they had a marshal and deputies and the place had been somewhat tamed. But one day there was a terrible event that shook the people of the bluffs. It was nearing election time and hostilities arose as they often do in politics. The brawl began in the Bar S Saloon when two liquored-up guys, let's call them Curly and Mortimer, got into a huge argument. Fists flew. Guns were drawn. Marshal Gannon walked into the place to calm the ruckus. Curly's gun discharged right into Marshal Gannon's chest, narrowly missing his tin star.

"Let's hang that coward, Curly Brown," shouted one of the bystanders. Others pounced on the startled man who was just coming to the shocking realization that he had just killed one of the most respected men in the county. The mob grabbed Curly and was on its way to hang him from a large old cottonwood on the edge of town when Mrs. Allgood rode up on her filly.

"Halt!" she cried. "This man deserves a fair trial. We have had enough bloodshed in this town for one day!" She convinced them to take Curly to the little jail behind the marshal's office. You see, Mrs. Allgood had considerable influence in the town as she was the wife of one of the wealthiest merchants. Also, she was exercising her conscience as a God-fearing, peace-loving kind of woman.

Under cover of dark that night, Mrs. Allgood had made arrangements for Curly to be sneaked onto the train to Falls City, a town about ten miles to the west. Curly was given his fair trial and served his time in jail. After he was released, he returned to live out his days in Rulo.

Marshal Gannon had been a good friend of Rouleau, who was now in his twilight years, and Gannon's demise troubled the old man greatly. He also felt that his beloved little city had been besmeared by the tragedy.

The townsfolk claimed he often went to the Bar S, where blood still stained the wooden floor, and he would have a drink and mourn his missing friend. Within a year, Rouleau joined Gannon in the cemetery on the top ridge of the bluffs.

But the spirit of old man Rouleau still patrols the streets of his little town, a town that has shrunk mightily in recent decades. They who still live there say that on nights when the mists roll up from the Big Muddy River and flood First Street, a dark figure emerges from the vapor and moves toward the old Bar S.

Two Haunting Ladies Of The Staircases

The remarkable Captain Molly so loved her riverboat steamship that it has long been reported that she never left it, even after her death in 1949 at the age of 80. Many passengers and officers of the Princess Queen report seeing, if not her physical body, her spiritual body on the lovely craft which she and her husband had bought in 1946.

Mary and Gordon Greene were married in 1890 and immediately established a steamboat line. The tiny, vivacious Mary convinced her husband that if he would take her on as a co-pilot, they could save money. She was probably the first woman who became certified to operate a ship alone.

The Greens prospered and eventually were owners of more than a dozen boats when they bought the prestigious Princess Queen, royalty of the river. Her historical pedigree included moving military men on the western river system during WWII. Later, the Princess Queen became the darling of tourist excursions and enthralled celebrities such as Princess Margaret of England, and President and Mrs. Jimmy Carter. The historic décor included a hardwood staircase and gilded woodwork; the crystal chandeliers and velvet curtains were indicative of the luxurious accommodations.

Indeed, Mary Greene, affectionately known as Captain Molly, loved her steamboat so much that she lived on it even as a retiree, seldom going ashore. In the years after her death, the "Princess Queen," reportedly, is still haunted by her spirit. A short, stout apparition, who is friendly and helpful, has been spotted on many occasions. An officer claims she was the presence that awakened him one night and impressed upon him that he should check the boat's vital areas. He found a leaking pipe which could have been disastrous had it gone on a few hours longer.

In another instance, a tour conductor on the boat said that a squatty little lady dressed in old-fashioned clothing often joined her tours. Why had this old lady signed on for so many excursions? Sometime later, after the tour director realized that she was actually Captain Molly, the mysterious lady no longer showed up on her tours.

Another couple claimed that Captain Molly brought them together. One night a young purser received a phone call from an elderly lady who said she was sick and needed help. She identified herself as a lady who had visited the purser's office earlier in the day. When the purser went to the designated room, she found it empty. She enlisted an officer to help her search for the caller. The two of them were in the corridors when the purser, a young lady, stopped in amazement before a portrait in the hallway. "That's her!" she exclaimed.

"Oh, that explains it!" said the officer. "That's Mrs. Greene." And he explained to the purser how Captain Molly had often made her appearances, and always in helpful ways. She was not a ghost to be feared.

A relationship between the purser and the officer was born that night and they claim that Captain Molly was the matchmaker. They were eventually married aboard the "Princess Queen" with a smiling Molly watching from the grand staircase.

Another lesser-known ghost of the grand staircase on the steamship was the lovely Hannah Jefferson. Often she has been spotted in a flowing white gown, an enigmatic smile playing upon her lips with most of her face hidden under a wedding veil.

Hannah was the daughter of Captain J.E. Jefferson, the severe and demanding master of the "River Queen," a prominent and proud ship among the hundreds plowing the many miles of the Missouri River in 1870.

Unlike her father, Hannah was a fun-loving and amiable young woman who often accompanied her father on the "River Queen," leaving the home of an aunt in St. Louis who had been her surrogate mother ever since the death of her own mother when Hannah was a young girl.

The captain's daughter with her laughing brown eyes and bouncing dark curls, was a joy to behold, and entranced passengers and crew alike.

One young man, a boisterous and dashing roustabout named Abraham Perl, took special notice of the captain's daughter, joining her in walks on the promenade deck and in merry dances in the ballroom where the ship's band played late into the night. It became quite apparent to all aboard that the twosome had fallen in love.

The captain got wind of it and declared Abraham unfit for his only child. "I forbid you to be seen with that black-hearted devil. He has no business, anyway, mingling with the first class passengers on the upper deck!"

"But, Father, Abe is off duty when we socialize. Why are you so opposed to him? He is really very dear, polite and kind, and he makes me laugh! Please, please give him a chance!"

"He'll never amount to a rat's a—. He's brash and uncouth. He's not fit to be courting any daughter of mine!" and the captain stormed from her stateroom, his heavy boots clomping on the wooden deck and then fading into the distance.

Hannah threw herself upon the satin comforter of her bed and wept.

Little did Hannah know that her father's hatred of Abraham stemmed from an event that occurred a year earlier when the two had become involved in a scuffle at the Saltwood Bar in the port town of Leavenworth. Abraham had out-fisted the captain in front of a large crowd, much to the captain's chagrin and humiliation. Despite the altercation, the captain had retained the young man because he was strong and performed well on the dock moving cargo. But the prospect of Abraham joining his family was a different matter entirely, and he would not abide it!

As the captain stood at the tiller wheel, the boat chugging through the gathering darkness, he made up his mind to dismiss Abraham at the next river call which would be Atchison.

Hannah avoided her father, missing the evening meal in the grand saloon. Instead, she caught up with Abraham as he stood smoking at the rail in the stern of the ship. There, with noise of the water as it splashed over the paddle wheel, the young lovers plotted their future.

Accordingly, Abraham was told his services were no longer required as the steamboat edged into the Atchison dock. He was to gather his things and leave the boat. The next day, another roustabout named Ivan informed Captain Jefferson that Abraham had promptly found a position on the "Flying Fremont," a faster steamship which was following and gaining on the "River Queen." The news infuriated the captain, who didn't want that "black-hearted devil" anywhere near his daughter.

"Go to the boiler room," he commanded the informer, "and tell them to pour on the wood, build up the steam! I'm not letting that devil anywhere near my daughter!"

Ivan did as he was told, but the "Flying Fremont" was still gaining on the "River Queen."

"Drat it!" yelled the captain. "Tell those firemen that I need more steam. We're coming to the Highland Straits (a narrow, fast-flowing channel among sandbars and snags). We'll bully that blankety-blank boat out of the road. Full steam ahead!"

Ivan's heart was racing. The captain was pushing the "River Queen" too hard. What was the matter with him anyway? One of the ships wasn't going to make it through those straits. The steam rose in great billowing clouds into the moonlight as the two ships raced toward the narrow pass.

In the annals of time, let it be written that Captain Jefferson won the race, and lost much more. We wonder if he enjoyed the moment when, across the dark ribbon of water, he saw the ball of fire and watched the "Flying Fremont" slowly sink into the depths. Was it vengeance enough to satisfy him when he heard that almost everyone on board had died? And how did he feel when he learned that his darling Hannah had also left his steamship that day in Atchison, that she had run with Abraham to the "Flying Fremont" where they had been welcomed aboard and were hoping to be married by Captain Ellis?

One of the few passengers who escaped the burning "Fremont" spoke of a dark-haired young girl who descended the grand staircase in a borrowed wedding gown and took the hand of an adoring young man only moments before the ship blew up. She supposed the captain was due to meet them there at the foot of the staircase to pronounce their vows, but he had been detained by urgent matters.

And thus another apparition of an earlier decade than the one of Captain Molly was seen on a grand staircase. The first a pleasant occurrence, the second a sad appearing of a young girl who haunted her father until his dying day, and in her pale wedding gown, haunts still the decks and staircase of the "River Queen."

In Love And War – The Baker House

The Baker House near Danville, Missouri, has long been a site of historic interest. Mr. Baker, the owner of the house during the Civil War, was a Union sympathizer. If not for the exploit of a young Rebel, the house would have undoubtedly been burned to the ground during a raid by Confederate soldiers. With his guerilla band, "Bloody Bill" Anderson approached the house which is situated north of the Missouri River in Montgomery County.

"Bloody Bill" had a mission in mind and that was to kill Mr. Baker because of his Northern sympathies. Finding him not at home, the guerillas trashed the fine old house, especially the women's bedrooms, a kind of "symbolic rape" in those war years. Many in that unit entered the house on horseback, riding roughshod through the rooms.

On this particular day, the guerillas set fire to Mrs. Baker's mattress before galloping off to their next plundering.

The story goes that one young man in the raiding party (who may have been the beneficiary of Mr. Baker's reputed kindness and generosity previously, or perhaps was an extended family member or neighbor) returned alone to the Baker home shortly thereafter. He is said to have taken an infant (who, for some reason, had been overlooked when the occupants escaped) out to a far spot in the yard and set the child down. Then he ran back into the smoke-filled house and put out the fire.

Toward evening of that same day, a young Southern cavalryman was given permission to take a meal with his family near Readsville. He was to return to duty within two hours. Johnny Powell was a lanky nineteen-year-old who had been fighting for the Southern cause for nearly a year, ever since his father had been killed by Union forces in the siege of Osceola, Missouri. Though their family had never owned slaves, the Powells were tied by heritage to Southern roots and sympathies.

His mother hadn't been expecting Johnny for supper that evening, but she exclaimed with delight when she looked through a front window and saw him ride up on his horse. "Johnny's home! I'll fry up some extra grits and ham. He's sure to be hungry for a home-cooked meal!"

At the name of her beloved brother, Sissy sprang to her feet and flew through the screen door.

"Johnny! Johnny! Can you stay a few days?"

Johnny jumped down from his horse, grabbed his sister around the waist and whirled her around. "Only here for a few hours. I've got to be back for bivouac at our camp south of here on the Big Mo."

"Ah, Johnny, I wish you could stay longer. You're looking thin! My, but it's so good to see you!"

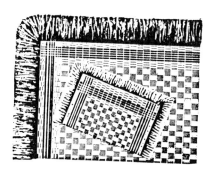

After Johnny washed up at the well outside, he came into the comfort of his boyhood kitchen and pulled up a chair. Ma and Sissy scurried about setting the table with the old familiar blue and white Wedgwood china. Ma and Sissy's chairs scraped on the floor as they also pulled up to the table. "For these gifts which you have given out of the abundance of Your goodness, we give You thanks, O Lord," they prayed.

Sissy offered the bowl of grits and ham to Johnny, who dug in with gusto.

"If we'd known you were comin', we'd a had your special apple cobbler," said his mother, smiling happily to have her son at her table again.

"That's alright, Ma. I'm just glad to be getting' these good grits. If we're near the home of one of the cavalrymen, ol' Anderson will lighten up and let us take a meal with our folks. But generally, he's a harsh ol' cuss. Reckon they don't call him 'Bloody Bill' for nothin'."

"Johnny," his mother beseeched him, "I hope you aren't gettin' to be as hard and bloody as he is, fer ridin' with him!"

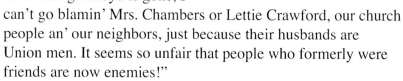

"There's a war out there, Ma, and sometimes we have to leave our better side behind us. The Yankees killed my father – your husband! Don't forget that, even for a minute!"

"Oh, I know, I know, but this is such a terrible war – families split apart in their loyalties. Even though Lloyd is gone, I can't go blamin' Mrs. Chambers or Lettie Crawford, our church people an' our neighbors, just because their husbands are Union men. It seems so unfair that people who formerly were friends are now enemies!"

"That's war, Ma. It's kill or be killed. The North started it all, and we ain't about to lie down and let the Union walk over us!"

"But Johnny, don't let hate and vengeance harden your soul. I pray for you every night, that you will be safe and that war won't embitter you."

"Just keep prayin', Ma."

All too soon it was time for Johnny to ride out. He hugged his mother tightly and told her not to worry. Sissy ran out to his horse with him.

"You know what, Johnny? My friend Elvira rode over just before you came. She said some unknown Reb rode back to the Baker house up by Danville and put out a fire and saved a baby. Wasn't that a lovely thing?"

"Could be dangerous for that rider…Bloody Bill wouldn't hesitate to shoot him for a traitor!" Johnny whispered, a concerned look on his face.

"Well, Elvira says it was the Baker house ghost who saved the day!"

"Sissy, do you believe in ghosts?" Johnny's eyes twinkled.

"I don't know…but I do believe in angels! I saw the soot on you when you rode in, before you washed up at the well!"

"Probably got too near the ashes of a campfire," Johnny hugged his sister and jumped up into the saddle.

"Goodbye, Johnny, I love you…and don't worry, your secret is safe with me!"

Johnny blew her a kiss as he headed his horse toward the Big Mo.

The Haunted "First Mansion"

The setting was the governor's mansion in Jefferson City, Missouri, and the year was 1983. A repairman had been working all day in the attic of the lovely old house built in 1871.

The repairman, we'll call him Mr. Jones, came down from the attic around 5:00 p.m., reporting to the staff that he had completed most of the work but would have to come back the next day to finish up. The governor of Missouri at the time was Christopher Bond, and it's important to this story to note that the Bonds had no young daughters living with them in the mansion.

Mr. Jones was unaware of this when he said to the Chief of Staff, "Do you think you ought to make the Bond family aware that their little girl was playing around in the attic, hanging out with me most of the day?"

"That's interesting. They don't have a little girl...I wonder who it could have been?" replied the Chief.

"Perhaps she belonged to one of the neighbors or was a daughter of one of the staff who works here…the cooks, maids or gardeners?"

"No little girl has been seen around here in the past few years! What did she look like?"

"Oh, she was around eight years old or so. She kept dancing around me in a kind of old-fashioned white dress, asking questions and chatting on and on. She was a cute little gal with blond curly hair."

The staff at the mansion was called together, and they mounted a search in all the rooms and closets, under staircases and in attics, but no one caught even a glimpse of a little blonde girl.

"I wonder," said the Chief of Staff reflectively to Mr. Jones, who was still there awaiting news of the little girl, "did you happen to see that fountain ornament when you came to the mansion this morning?"

"Yeah, I admired the workmanship on the bronze figure of a child merrily dancing in the spray of the water. A right nice ornament that caught my attention!"

"Well, that is said to be Carrie Crittenden, who was the nine-year-old daughter of Governor Thomas Crittenden. She died a hundred years ago, in 1883."

"Really!" Mr. Jones' eyes widened. "Why did she die?" Mr. Jones had never really given much credence to ghosts and the supernatural, but now he became rather spooked.

"Governor Crittenden ran his campaign on a promise to rid the state of all unlawful activity going on. He cracked down against bandit and guerilla activity. Supposedly he had something to do with Robert Ford killing Jesse James. At least,

he ended up pardoning him after a jury found Ford guilty. Anyway, Crittenden had a lot of enemies among the outlaws of the state, and they were a ruthless bunch."

"Yes, I remember reading from my schoolbooks about those wild days in Missouri history."

"Anyway, Governor Crittenden's life was threatened, as well as his daughter's. The governor hired bodyguards to protect his beloved child. But all was in vain, for she died anyway. After her passing, her father wrote and published a song 'My Child' and had Carrie's figure cast in bronze so she could forever dance on the front lawn."

"Did someone gun her down?" asked the incredulous Mr. Jones.

"No, it was a much more treacherous invader who killed her, one no bodyguard could save her from...she died of diphtheria!"

"Really! What a sweet and lovely child she was, if that's who kept me company in the attic all day."

"So many children died of diphtheria in those years, estimates are in the thousands. Well, thank you, Mr. Jones, for the work you did today...we'll pay you tomorrow when you finish up."

But the nervous Mr. Jones collected his tools, walked quickly past the dancing girl on the fountain, and never returned to the mansion.

The Gambler And The Rose

Arrow Rock, Missouri, settled in 1815, was a booming commercial port in the early nineteenth century. At one time it had a population of over a thousand people, boosted at times by many thousand more steamboat travelers and river workers.

Famous Missourians who have been raised in Arrow Rock or dwelled there for a time include three state governors, the painter George Caleb Bingham and Dr. John Sappington, a man whose research led to a cure for malaria.

Although there are now fewer than a hundred residents, this historical little river town boasts a lyceum theater, antique and gift shops, restaurants and bed and breakfasts in restored old Victorian homes. And, as is true of so many old river towns, ghosts flock there like moths to streetlamps.

One notable place for poltergeist activity is The Old Tavern. The landmark was built by the slaves of a southerner named John Huston. The main floor of the tavern is still used as a restaurant, but rumors of ghosts have kept many from going up to the second level, including a very frightened servant girl who was cleaning on the second floor and said she saw a ghost and promptly quit her job.

One of the more recent managers of the restaurant is Bunny Thomas who reports that once she heard her name called out. She turned and there was no one there.

Another time late at night, Bunny said she entered the dining room which was empty at the time, and heard a man's voice call out in a flirtatious manner, "Well, hello there!"[1]

The question arises, what traumatic event happened at this old tavern that still troubles a roving spirit? Some believe that it is the ghost of Basil Bowdoin, a former boarder and poker player extraordinaire. He was first a gambler on the steamboats, but had drifted ashore and set up shop in The Old Tavern. It seems Basil had run out of luck in a strange occurrence on the second floor of this venerable old building.

Another erstwhile resident at The Old Tavern at this time was a once-lovely gal called Belle Rose. She wore her make-up heavy and her clothing tight, preferring short, tightly laced satin dresses. Her coy smile and the swing in her hips made her a favorite among the clientele. Her trademark was a satin rose she always wore in her wavy, black hair.

Basil and Belle were quite a duo. At first, there may have been some romance in their relationship, but their penchant for fine things, be it fancy cigars and fine booze, or elegant suits and dresses, the couple soon realized that they would make better business partners than lovers.

At the poker table, Basil cut quite a figure with a black string tie, polished black boots and precisely trimmed mustache. Everyone soon knew him as "The Gambler." And the odd thing is this – even though they knew that he knew when to "hold 'em and when to fold 'em," they still couldn't resist pulling up a chair and anteing up.

"Hey, Belle, bring a round of beer for my comrades here," Basil would call in his rich baritone voice, pulling out some bills for the tab.

Belle Rose would flounce over to the table with foaming mugs. "Here ya go, Buster, bottoms up," she'd wink at the lambs being wooed for the slaughter.

"Belle Rose, you're the pride of the Missouri," Basil would flirt, and she would curtsy in return as she made her way back to the bar for more drinks, the cameo locket, big as a pocket watch, bouncing on her chest. She was never without that locket.

As she rounded the table, she touched her extravagant piece of jewelry, the white ivory bust of Belle's good luck piece, behind the chair of Chester Banks, a message subtly sent to Basil. Thus, "the luck" had been enhanced by a refined set of signals.

In return for these favors, Basil sent many paying customers to Room 3 at the top of the stairs. After a flourishing night of poker and "more," Basil and Belle split the take.

For a while, everyone at The Old Tavern was as happy as duckies on a pool, and then things started "going south." Basil greedily accused Belle of holding out on him. "Hey, lady, I lay all my cards on the table, but are you? Where are you stashing the extra loot?"

"Simmer down, Buster! You're getting all that's coming to you!"

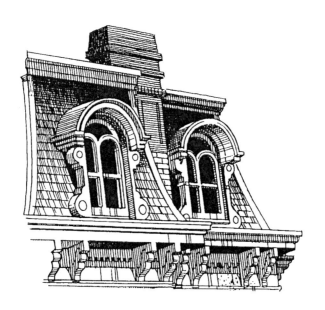

"All that's coming to me! What the devil does that mean?" he roared as he took a menacing step toward her. "What's in that big old watchcase you wear around your neck, anyway? Did you convert some of the cash into gold nuggets, and hide them in there? You've been taking more than your share, I've a mind!" and he reached for her chest.

"You fool! Keep your hands off me and my locket!" Belle backed away from him in her room on the second floor. The window toward the street was wide open. Basil lunged for the locket. Belle, reflexes still acute, stepped aside. Basil's boot caught in a fold of the rag rug and catapulted him headlong out the window. The coroner was called and he wrote the cause of death as a broken neck. There was some speculation around Arrow Rock that Belle had pushed the unfortunate gambler to his death, but, of course, that could never be proved.

But the circumstances of his demise may explain to whom that bodiless voice belonged that called out to Bunny in the empty dining room. Just maybe it would explain the scraping of furniture, the footsteps, the sound of slamming windows and doors, and all the other noises in the night. And maybe, it would also explain why a red rose can sometimes be found on the floor by the window of Room Number 3 in The Old Tavern.

[1] Gilbert, Joan, Missouri Ghosts, Mogho Books, 2001, pg. 145.

The Devil And The Gargoyles

Once a booming and wealthy town, Atchison, Kansas, is now known as one of the most haunted places in Kansas. Sitting aloft the towering bluffs of the Missouri River are numerous extravagant Victorian houses, many of which are now on the National Historic Register. These houses are evidence of the wealth of old-time railroad magnates, bankers and hardware outfitters for the wagon trains headed west.

The McInteer Villa on Kansas Avenue is one example. It was built by John McInteer, an Irish immigrant whose harness making business catapulted him into riches. His ode to success is a fabulously ornate house with many gables, balconies and porches…a monument to the American dream. Ghosts have also come to live in grand style in the Villa. One of the odd phenomenon is the lights which turn on and off in the tower – which does not have electricity wired to it! Some people have taken pictures within the house and when the film is developed, figures appear in the background. Figures have also been seen standing in windows when the house is vacant. This is one of the houses which is on the haunted house tour sponsored by the Chamber of Commerce of Atchison.

On another street in this proud old city is a mansion that was built by J.P. Wesley (an alias to protect a family name) who was a banker, politician and entrepreneur. J.P. was born into a family of modest means and he became driven to rise above his humble roots.

As the age-old story goes, he took the shortest and surest route to success – he made a deal with the devil. Those deals aren't too hard to broker – he'll give you the best of worldly pleasure but upon your death your soul belongs to him.

J.P., through a series of inordinately fortunate events and rapscallion deals, rose to prominence in Atchison. He founded a bank, but gave loans with high interest rates (usury) and would promptly foreclose without a drop of compassion. He padded his portfolio upon the backs of the common people. He even dabbled in politics where shenanigans of various kinds are performed.

In the 1880s, he and his wife, Miranda, commissioned a famous architect to design a home that would be a veritable showcase of wealth. The home featured parquet floors – all the rage at the time – and molded, elegant ceiling decorations. One of its most distinctive features was a grand staircase with marble stairs.

Since this was about the time of J.P.'s fiftieth birthday, he was growing more cognizant of his life's dwindling days, and he became more troubled as he thought about the devil coming for him. Maybe he could somehow cheat even the old Master Cheater.

So J.P., hearing that many European edifices contained gargoyles as guardians, was determined they should be indispensable in his new home. These grotesque creatures were said to keep evil away, even the devil himself. These ugly creatures from Gothic realms were often carved in stone or molded in lead. J.P ordered the most grotesque creatures he could find to be placed atop the highest roof ridges.

Meanwhile, he said to his wife, "Miranda, it's time you and I started back to church! And we'll take along a big sack of money for the collection plate…some back offerings I'm bound to pay."

"Whatever you say, J.P., but it's likely it won't change the mind of the devil much at all and may just make Old Scratch laugh," Miranda scorned, waving her diamond bedecked fingers in the air.

69

So J.P. went off to church. He sang hymns loud and long but it wouldn't drown out the chuckling of the devil in his ear.

One day, Miranda suggested something else which might help. "J.P., why don't you join the WCTU (the Women's Christian Temperance Union). You could sign that pledge to not touch a drop of alcohol." So her husband took her advice and readily signed the pledge on the day that he also gave a handsome donation to the union. From then on, he left off the spirits, and all he ever drank was a little "fortified" grape juice.

"It's not enough, Miranda," he said one day. "It's the breath of the devil I've been feeling – he's breathing hot and heavy down my neck."

"I had a dream last night that you should do something for all the people you may have wronged on your way up," she replied.

"Bully for you, my clever wife, what a grand idea! I know what I'll do. I'll build a fountain for the people so they can come and be refreshed by the water we'll pump out of the Missouri River. They can catch the water drops on their tired and sweaty faces!"

"Yes, and it will be a monument to us. We'll have our names engraved on a golden plaque at its base."

70

"Of course, of course!"

One would have thought that after all these precautions, J.P would have been able to sleep nights, but not so. He started having nightmares, kicking wildly at unseen forces and crying out with shrill screams. After such a ruckus, Miranda's sleep was also disturbed.

"There! There! Do you see that horrendous thing in the window? It's him! It's him! There's a giant beast and blood's dripping down its face! Oh, horrors! Horrors!"

Miranda tried to quiet him. "J.P., there is nothing in the windows, only the gargoyles on the balcony roof."

"No, no, it's real! It's the devil's face! Oh, my heart, my heart!

It's quaking unto death!" he said as he clutched his chest.

After a few more torturous nights, Miranda moved to another one of their many bedrooms, one which was much further down the hall. One night she heard so much commotion in J.P.'s wing of the house that she ran to his room and saw a most amazing sight!

J.P. was stomping about in his nightshirt. He had on his riding boots and a Conquistador hat on his head with an iron fire poker in his hand. "Get out! Get out!" he yelled as he lunged the poker through the windows, crashing glass all over the velvet carpet. He turned to face his wife with blood dripping from every orifice. He raised the hand that had been shredded by the glass from the window and grasped his throat before he fell to the

floor. His body began writhing and he began foaming at the mouth. His eyes were glazed with terror. Within minutes he died.

Miranda heard a fiendish laugh that seemed to emanate from a gargoyle just outside the window. "Oh, my God," she shuddered as she backed out of the room. "The devil got his due!"

For weeks after his death, Miranda heard loud noises and screams from J.P.'s former bedroom – it seemed he was still jousting with the devil, even after death.

She couldn't take any more of this now haunted house, and she packed up one day and moved away.

The mansion stood empty for a few years until a man by the name of Halsey, who made a fortune in his brick factory, offered to buy it from Miranda. Halsey had found a way to fire the clay from the Missouri River banks into millions of bricks which were selling like the proverbial "hot cakes." They were in great demand for building the elegant houses and for paving the hilly streets of Atchison.

Halsey said that he didn't believe all that hocus-pocus about ghosts and gargoyles. But once he moved into the mansion, his personality started to change. He, just like the resident who preceded him, started to become involved in some questionable activities. Then his health started to fail. He suffered bouts of gout, chilblains and stomach ulcers. His beloved dog, Oodles, died, and his wife, Tillie, ran away with the iceman.

As he watched his life crumble, he reopened the ghost room which he had sealed off when he moved in. He saw the gargoyle out the window, leering at him from its rooftop perch.

"That's the trouble. It's the gargoyles. I'll get rid of them and my life will turn around." So he ran down the marble staircase and to the carriage house where he found a saw and hammer to accomplish the removal of those fiendish gargoyles.

But he slipped on the stairs as he rushed back up, and with a few thuds and a final clunk, he fell to his death!

Since then, the neighbors have heard the slamming and banging of doors and windows, and they swear that not one, but two, ghosts now inhabit the old Victorian house.

And if you go by it at night and you look hard at the roof, you'll see those gargoyles with their hideous grins, and you may see the blood that runs down their faces and drips from their chins. Whatever you do, run as fast as you can when you see the fiery glow in their eyes.

The One-Armed Man Of Haunted Hollow

Perhaps one of the most haunted places in Nebraska is Indian Cave State Park, which includes the old river town settlement of St. DeRoin. People from both sides of the Missouri River flock to this state park, not only for the breathtaking scenery which melts to burnished gold, red and amber hillsides in autumn, but they also love this place for its ghost appeal.

Especially in October! That's when all the camping pads are booked far in advance for two amazing, spooktacular weekends. Up to fifty people dress as ghosts and populate the winding lanes of the park for the annual hayrack rides. One area of the park is known as "Haunted Hollow," a dark and creepy basin that many do believe is inhabited by spirits, real-live ghosts and not just dress-up ghosts for the weekend.

Longtime park employee and resident historian, Cheryl McDowell, who works in the blacksmith shop, one of the Living History features of the park, admits that it can really be spooky down in Haunted Hollow after dark. She is a delightful storyteller who entertains those who visit her blacksmith shanty with many true stories about the history of the region, and she's also an expert in ghost lore.

One of the most popular stories that she tells concerns A.J. Ritter, an early father of old St. DeRoin. He was a colorful character who basically owned the town. He was the judge and, at one time, a sheriff. He built the lumberyard, the sawmill and the warehouse. He had three children and saw to the erection of a schoolhouse.

On top of all this, old A.J. owned the general store and pharmacy. Up in the hills beyond the store he had a "still" and manufactured snake oil which he sold under the counter at his general store. Snake oil, being heavily braced with alcohol, was good for whatever might ail a man. It was medicinal as well as recreational.

One day, old A.J. decided to go fishing on the Missouri River in a little rowboat. Now it must be noted that in those days before the Army Corps of Engineers channeled the river so it ran deeper and faster, the big old Missouri was a lazier river, slow and wide and a good place for a rowboat and fishing net.

On this particular lovely fall afternoon, A.J. gathered some supplies from his store for a leisurely outing. He took two bottles of snake oil, a cigar, a rope and a few sticks of dynamite. Yes, he stocked dynamite in his store for the use of the farmers who were clearing their land.

He rowed out into the middle of the river, taking snorts of snake oil all the way. By the time he was ready to begin fishing, he had already downed one of the bottles of snake oil. He tied up a couple of sticks of the dynamite with the rope. His cigar was conveniently lit, so he touched it to the fuses of the dynamite, standing up in the boat so he could toss the bundle into the mainstream, but he was by this time quite tipsy and he stumbled backwards.

Realizing the sizzling fuses were soon going to detonate the bomb, he threw it straight up in the air to get rid of it! A poor reaction, for the loaded missile came straight down again, exploding in the crease of his elbow. It blew off most of his arm.

A.J. looked down at the dangling chunk of meat and sobered up in record time. He immediately made a tourniquet out of his handkerchief and somehow, using his one good arm, got the boat rowed back to the shore.

He ran up the path to the doctor's office. Dr. Lorenzo Rice is buried in the St. DeRoin cemetery for anyone who wants to ascertain that such a person really existed.

When A.J. arrived with bloody arm swinging loosely, he called, "Dr. Rice, it's an emergency – help me at once!"

Dr. Rice, who had his back to the door and was busy sewing up a farmer's wound, just kept sewing. Without even looking around, the doctor said, "A.J., I can smell your breath! Sit down and I'll get to you."

A.J. came to face the doctor, flinging out his mangled arm. Supposedly, the doctor deadpanned, "Yes, you do have a bit of a problem."

So he clipped the thread of the farmer's wound and saw to A.J. immediately. "Wheedle dee dee, A.J., there's not much I can do. I certainly can't reattach this sorry limb! I will have to amputate."

All of the above is documented as historical truth, but here is where the story gets hazy:

Dr. Rice didn't know what to do with the detached arm after A.J. left his office that afternoon. So he finally decided to wrap it in a towel and bury it. After dusk he took it to the far end of town and buried it under a big old sycamore tree.

A few weeks later, the disgruntled Mr. Ritter met the doctor on the street. "You're a quack! You're a worthless doctor! I can still feel my arm and it's riddled with pain. I'm grumpy and I growl at my wife and my kids! I'm just not fit to be out with people and it's all your fault!"

The doctor took A.J. to his office and examined him. "I don't see anything wrong. Your stub is healing well."

"But I hurt! My arm just throbs it hurts so damn much!"

"Well, let me consult my medical books." The doctor excused himself to his small office. After a while, he came back to the examining room. "A.J., I think I've found it…you have 'phantom arm syndrome.' Your body thinks your arm is still attached. Come with me; we'll dig up your arm and maybe that will help you." Of course, the doctor meant that it would psychologically relieve the ailing man.

When they dug up the arm, the hand was clenched in a fist. "See, that's the problem." The doctor opened up the hand, and lo and behold, A.J. instantly felt better, and left once again without claiming his arm.

Now Dr. Rice stood there perplexed. Should he rebury it here under this tree or further down the riverbank, or should he take it up to the cemetery. Well, he ended up planting it somewhere in an undisclosed location.

That turned out to be a big problem for A.J., for he died sometime later, and though his body has now turned to dust, he isn't at rest without his missing arm. People say they have seen the figure of a one-armed man on certain moonlit nights walking up and down by the riverbank in "Haunted Hollow." And most everyone just naturally assumes that it is A.J. Ritter looking for his arm.

Steamboat's A-Comin'

Jeremiah Stanton was a ne'er-do-well farmer who nudged his old horse just enough to plow an insubstantial living out of his Missouri tobacco farm. Charlena was his high-toned wife from back east. Their marriage had produced two sons, Charles, 15, and Lawrence, 13.

Though one wonders how Charlena had ever been charmed by a rough-handed, heavy-booted hill farmer, it seems their eyes met one night at a social in the town hall. Charlena was in Missouri visiting cousins and having a good time. Starlight and homebrew under a full moon must have dulled their senses, but soon silks were exchanged for calico, and Charlena became Jeremiah's partner in trying to eke out an existence from the soil.

"Jeremiah," she would beseech, "let's plow up that north slope, and put in more crops!"

"Nah, that's full of native grass and stones – wouldn't amount to much no how."

"Jeremiah Stanton, how did I ever marry such a no-account! We're never going to get ahead!" Indeed, Charlena had not forgotten her days of silks and furs, parasols and teas.

"Have you washed my other pair of overalls – the ones with the cow manure? Go on, woman, you've got more pressing things to do than keep bellerin' at me."

The sons slinked off to the barn to escape the continuous bickering between their ill-matched parents.

Primary among Charlena's harpings was her desire that Jeremiah should get an apprenticeship on a steamboat so he could learn to be a river pilot. It was 1858 and steam boating on the Missouri River was a thriving business. What's more, it was romantic and colorful and flamboyant! The whistle of the steamboat as it neared a port was the call of enchantment. Almost everyone in the river towns would hasten to the dock to watch the unloading of passengers and cargo.

The crew of a steamboat was envied and respected, especially the pilot and captain. Truly the pilots of those huge machines were the rock stars of their day. All the young boys longed to grow up and become, if not a pilot, a fireman or roustabout on a steamboat.

"We could be rich!" Charlena whined. She reminded Jeremiah that captains could make over a thousand dollars a month, a princely sum, especially in contrast to the pittance that they wrested from the soil. Plying the waters of the Missouri, that would be their golden opportunity!

Jeremiah kept dousing her fantasies with cold water. "That's a darned dangerous trade, woman. What do you want me to do, go off and git myself killed! That old Missouri is full of fast currents and eddies, sandbars and snags from downed trees. It'd be foolhardy to be on one of them boats with boilers that like as not would blow up. Why, even some of the newer ones that have pressure gauges on them have blowed up, and the fireman aboard couldn't save the darn things – they sank, taking cargo and passengers to a muddy grave at the bottom of the river. Why, scads of them boats have already drowned."

But Charlena would not be silenced. It became her obsession, so finally Jeremiah gave in and went to Boonville to sign on with Captain LaFarge, a master and celebrity of his profession, to learn every crook and eddy, every bend and bar in that wild, unruly river. Jeremiah was older than most of the other apprentices who normally became riverboat pilots, but he dutifully kept his log and took his shifts, four hours in the

wheelhouse and four hours at rest, managing the broken sleep of those irregular hours. Reluctantly at first, he began memorizing every mile of the river from Boonville to Fort Benton, Montana, and surprised even himself by how adept a river man he was becoming. At the end of his apprenticeship, Captain LaFarge recommended him to the owner of the Belle of Boonville who was actually seeking out a mature pilot, instead of the younger fellows who were more inclined toward racing their steamboats against each other, blowing up the boilers and endangering the costly investments of the owners. Why, a steamship alone was usually worth $50,000 or more, disallowing the valuable cargo.

Charlena was overjoyed when her husband won his appointment. She bragged about the family's imminent riches up and down the main street of Boonville. She chided the dry goods merchant to import plenty of extravagant yard goods as she would be needing a whole new wardrobe. She eyed the jeweled combs and lace shawls and made a list of all she would buy when Jeremiah brought home his paycheck.

In the weeks before he left on his maiden voyage the following spring, Charlena approached Jeremiah, "Husband, why don't you take Charles and Lawrence with you? They are big, strong boys. They could be roustabouts, loading and unloading cargo. Think how much richer we could be!"

"What about runnin' the farm and puttin' in a crop?" he asked.

"Oh, don't worry about that. I'll hire old Stooley down the road to help me. I'd get by – but what an opportunity for our boys to travel and see new things and make more money than they could ever make here in the hills!"

"Woman, some of them roustabouts are pretty crude guys. You sure you want our boys carousing with the likes of them?"

"You'll be there to take care of them. They're good boys – they'll be all right!"

Actually, Charles and Lawrence were very inclined to leave the drudgery of the farm and set out on a riverboat adventure, and they joined their mother in nagging Jeremiah for their employment. So, in April of 1859, after the ice on the river had melted, Jeremiah, Charles and Lawrence threw rough homespun bags of their belongings over their shoulders and boarded the ill-fated Belle of Boonville.

Charlena stood on the dock, waving her sunbonnet at her departing family as the large wheel lifted its paddles through the murky water. She swelled with pride and visions of riches, but little did she know that this was her last sight of her husband and sons.

Just above Atchison, Kansas, the ship which had been caught in the turbulent waters of a spring storm, hit a snag and sank, taking with it a valuable load of cargo and a couple hundred passengers and crewmen, including her husband and sons.

As for Charlena, her dreams died with them. She became a bitter and lonely old woman, living out her days in near poverty. For many years after the sinking of the Belle, she would come to the docks, stand there breathing in the fishy smell of the place, scanning the horizon, listening for the whistle of a certain steamship.

"Listen," she'd say to nearby fishermen or port workers, "it's comin' around the bend. My dearly beloved Jeremiah is comin' back to me and he's bringin' my boys. See it! I see the steamboat; it's comin'! It's comin'! I see it! I see it!"

And believe it or not, for years after Charlena was dead and buried, many people in those parts professed to seeing the ghostly ship round that particular bend in the river with its great wheel churning up the waters of the Missouri, the river that had become the final resting place for hundreds of those old steamers.

From Iowa With Love

Jenny looked out her kitchen window, down the long slope and across a field that bordered the Missouri River. She sighed as she wrung out her dishcloth in a basin of water. More than anything she wanted to run out the door of the little farmhouse, swim that old muddy river and somehow fly 350 miles to be with her mother, Coleen, the Irish mother who had nurtured her with so much laughter and love.

The letter from Jenny's sister, Lizzie, in Iowa City read: "Come as soon as you can. Mother is not doing well. Dad is drinking heavily and is no help at all. Brother Peter is unable to leave his business in St. Louis."

"Oh, Mother, how I wish I could be there with you – I miss you so much it hurts!" But Jenny was stuck here on their little farm south of Arago, Nebraska, on the Missouri River. Just this morning her husband, Ed, had commiserated with her but allowed it just wouldn't be possible to send her and their four children to Iowa City right now. The spring floods had wiped

out their corn crop. There was barely enough money to buy
seed to replant.

"This stupid farm!" Jenny had stamped her foot at Ed, "all it
does is bring us misery. Will we ever get ahead?!"

"Now, Love, you know we have to be patient. Someday we'll
make the last payment and the farm will be ours. It's good,
rich soil. There's nothing better than river bottom land, and
someday it's going to be worth all the trouble, you wait and
see!"

"Why don't we trade for a different farm – one further away
from this horrible river? We're always at the mercy of the river!
We break our backs clearing the timber and urging the horses
on to plow enough to reap a few crops, and the next thing you
know, the river comes along lapping at our door, destroying our
dreams!"

"Now, now, Jenny, the river bottom land is far better than that
up on those rocky bluffs. It doesn't help that our country is in
the midst of this darn Depression, but things will get better."

"But my mother may not be!" and the tears started coursing down her cheeks. Ed took her in his arms and held her. At last, he took his straw hat from the peg by the door and left for the field. His walk was not as jaunty as usual. He was sorry he couldn't find a way for Jenny to go home to Iowa.

In the twelve years of their marriage, she had been able to return to her girlhood home twice. Once shortly after she and Ed were married, and once two years ago when the family had ridden across the Missouri River on the Iron Horse, boarding at Rulo, about 15 miles south of Arago.

The Rulo railroad bridge had been completed in 1889 at a cost of one million dollars and was the fastest way across the river. The automobile bridge was due to be opened in 1939, but that was several years away, and there wasn't a guarantee their old Ford could make it all the way to Iowa City even if the toll bridge was open today.

Jenny walked out to the henhouse to spread mash for the chickens. She glared down at the river – it maddened her to see it rolling inexorably along, unconcerned by her plight. That plague-gonnit river was a symbol, a long rope of water that hemmed her in. Ed loved the river, loved her many faces. "The river is like you, Jenny," he had said, "she's moody and changeable. Sometimes sparkling and laughing, sometimes dark and frowning, and sometimes all whipped up and foamy with tears."

"Ah, Ed, you're <u>so</u> romantic," she scowled on that day so long ago.

"And you are my little water sprite," he had countered as he lifted her and swung her around.

How had she gotten here, so far from the mother she adored? True, she had been young and restless. She wanted to see new places so she had applied to be a schoolteacher in Shenandoah, Iowa. Ed came to a Chautauqua event at the schoolhouse one night and the next thing Jenny knew, she was living on a farm in Nebraska.

Oh, she loved Ed. She wouldn't change that, and she loved her children, Eddie, Jack, Rose and baby Elsa. She loved them all dearly, and though the family had little in material goods, they did have food from the garden and animals, a roof over their heads, and they had each other. It was just that darned river!

A few days later, the mailman brought them their mail, driving up their long gravel lane. "There's a special delivery letter here for you, Mrs. Henderson. Thought I'd bring it on up to the house for you. Might be pretty important."

"Thank you, Cyrus," Jenny said as she took the envelope with trembling hands. It was from Lizzie. It must be bad news for one letter to follow so closely on the heels of another.

"Mother passed away early this morning. The funeral will be Friday. Wish you could be here to help with the arrangements. Love, Lizzie." Friday – that was today! Jenny threw her apron up to her face and collapsed in tears. She had missed the chance of seeing her mother alive again – and now she would miss her funeral, too! "Oh, Mother, Mother!" she cried as little Elsa clung to her leg and the older children scooted outside, awed to see their mother so overwhelmed.

That afternoon, Jenny stood at her sink gazing out over the Missouri, Old Misery, today for sure! She thought of the stately brick church in Iowa City where, at this moment, Preacher Wilton was performing her mother's funeral. She felt sad and guilty for not being there, but here she was, three hundred and fifty miles away with a huge wide river between!

Suddenly there was a presence in the kitchen with her – a warm and loving presence from behind and she actually heard her mother's voice, sweet and true: "It's all right, Jenny. I understand."

The burden was lifted. She had not been able to go to her mother, but her mother had come to her, across all those miles and the bounds of the universe. A sweet peace flooded over her. As she looked out the window again, she could see rays of sunlight filtering through the dark clouds and twinkling on the face of the Old Missouri.

The Gay Gadfly Of Atchison

"Papa, please hitch up the team to my carriage. The steamboat is coming from St. Louis with all the latest fashions in dresses and I want to be among the first to see them!" pronounced Annabel Lamour with a petulant toss of her long corkscrew curls.

"Now, now, Annabel. I have to meet a client at the bank at 1:00 and I just don't have time right now…I'm going to be late as it is," said Jeremiah Lamour as he wiped his beard-rimmed mouth with a linen dinner napkin and rose from his chair.

"But, Papa, please! I don't want to walk all the way down Ferry Street to the dock. I need my carriage, and I need it right now!"

"Shh! Quiet down, my darling daughter, don't fret so! If you simply must go to the dock this afternoon, a little constitutional might do you good." Jeremiah patted the pompadour of his only daughter, donned his top hat and gloves and left through the leaded glass door of his mansion on the highest bluff of Atchison, Kansas.

Today that scenic and historic town is considered one of the most haunted places in Kansas. It is full of fine old Victorian houses built by wealthy lumber merchants and railroad magnates of the past. The Atchison, the Topeka and the Santa Fe was just one of the many railroads in this busy hub on the western side of the Missouri River.

Notable also in its prominence on the map of history was Atchison's link to the California gold fields. Up to 1600 wagons a day were ferried across the river in 1849 and the 1850s. The hustle and bustle of the docks was colorful and exciting to all the people who came to witness the great exodus west.

Ferry Street was a steep street that ran straight down a tall hill and onto the dock. Since then, the roadway name has been changed to Atchison Street, and it is one of the many brick arteries of that fair city.

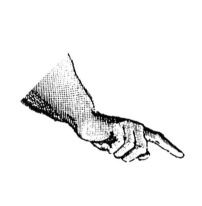

Annabel Lamour was quite the socialite in the booming days of this river city. When the servant girl saw how her spoiled mistress flounced from the table and headed toward the carriage house, she reported to Mabel, the cook, "That girl, she ain't gonna mind her daddy, I'll wager. He tole her to wait with hitchin' the team, and off she goes anyway!"

"Tsk, tsk," the cook replied, "I know it, I know it! Nothin' good's gonna come of all that spoilin'. Ever since her mother died five years ago, Mister Lamour, he jis lets that girl have anything she wants, and now she's like a headstrong colt that's just gonna go her own way."

Annabel had paused long enough after her repast to pick up her parasol from a stand near the mahogany table where the beautiful Tiffany lampshade cast colorful rainbows on the Oriental rug. She pulled on her driving gloves and cast an admiring glance at her image in the long mahogany-trimmed mirror before leaving.

Miss Annabel Lamour was a sight to behold. When she sashayed down the street, heads turned. Her sparkling brown eyes flashed "come hither" spells on all the young gentlemen. The flounces in her skirt bounced, as did the curls on her shoulders as she enticed the lads in their high polished boots and starched white collars. Indeed, she was a gay gadfly, the "toast of the town," the laughing belle of Atchison.

After a bit, the servant girl reported to the kitchen again. "She did it her own self! She hitched up the team, an' she's got the doors open to the carriage house. Oh, what should we do?"

"Nothin'! We have no rule over her so's let 'er go. She's bound to have her comeuppance one o' these days."

Soon they heard the clip clop of the horses' hooves as they passed the parlor windows, and the servants, running to the front of the house, saw their stubborn young mistress tearing in her carriage toward Ferry Street.

And then, just as she started down that long, fateful hill, something happened. She lost control of the horses, and they came unhitched from the carriage, probably they were ill hitched in the first place. Annabel screamed as the horseless carriage gathered speed, and still more speed. "Help me! Help me!" she cried as she zoomed under the low-hanging branches of the oak trees.

A few astonished pedestrians gazed in amazement at the flying apparition. One man came to his senses and tried to dash to her aid, but he might as well have tried to catch a comet by the tail.

The screaming girl in the horseless carriage flew to the end of Ferry Street and continued on, catapulting across the dock and into the dark, murky depths of the Missouri River!

Annabel's body never was recovered and to this day that portion of the riverbank in Atchison is said to be haunted. Men say they can hear a young woman's voice calling them to join her in the water...the gay gadfly, the "toast of the town," the mermaid of the ol' Missouri calls to them.

"Tumbling Blocks" On The Underground Railroad

Sophie wasn't accustomed to talking to what others of us would consider to be only an empty chair, but she did that day.

"Mother, tell me again, why is this quilt pattern so important to you?" said Sophie as she squinted to thread her needle.

"Well, as you know in these bloody times along the Kansas-Missouri border, this quilt will be a code for runaway slaves going north. This particular pattern is called 'tumbling blocks.' It will be put over a fence at a safe house, telling the escapees that there is an underground railroad agent in the area."

"I thought only the colored folks made these quilts as secret messages to other Negroes. For instance, the 'wrench pattern' meant to gather your tools and be prepared to escape."

"Oh, no, some of us abolitionist women joined their cause, though it is very dangerous. Helping slaves escape could be met with hanging in some southern states."

"I rather like this pattern. I've heard there are about ten in all."

"Yes, the one I especially like is the 'bear's paw.' It means to take a mountain trail and follow the paths of bear tracks – they most surely will lead you to water and food."

"Is there a deadline on this quilt? How long do we have to get it finished?"

"Well, Cousin Matilda wants it as soon as possible over there in Jackson County. You know it's very heavily pro-slavery over there and she aims to help the ones trying to get the Negroes to Canada. She's friends to John Brown. She's even helped him and his men find transport for the slaves across the Missouri River. You've surely heard of John Brown?"

"That I surely have! He's quite a fiery leader of the abolitionists – a wild man with a rifle in one hand and a Bible in the other, I've heard."

"I greatly admire him. Some just sit back and talk, but he <u>does</u>! I like a man who will fight for his convictions."

"Hiram hates him and, of course, all his pro-slavery family from over in Missouri hate him, too!"

"Oh, I know. How you ever got hitched up with that pro-slavery man, I'll never know! And here you are farming over here in the free state of Kansas – that's quite weird."

"Well, Hiram has never owned slaves and he was able to get a good buy on this forty acres, so here we are! But Hiram upholds his family in Missouri, who own slaves. He says it's a biblical right. He cites that scripture about being fair to your slaves…like it's an endorsement of slavery."

"Oh, pshaw, that's no excuse a'tall of making your brother be in submission to you. We are all God's children and he loves us all the same."

"Mother, you're preaching to the choir! I believe that!"

"And what's more, I have two daughters, you and Lizzie. You have blue eyes and Lizzie has brown eyes and I love you both the same. Neither one of you is better than the other or should mistreat the other!"

"Calm down, I know that, Mother. Hiram will come in from the field and hear you ranting so!"

"Don't care if he does!"

"By the way, it's probably a deep secret, but do you know the route of the Underground Railroad?"

"Well, the first stop is at Quindaro when they cross the river and then they go to Lawrence, then comes Topeka and then on to Nebraska. Many of our sisters and brothers in the cause have stations or safe houses along the route where slaves can receive food and shelter."

"I've heard there's a cave under a cabin up around Nebraska City near the river."

"Sure enough. It's actually a cave under a pioneer cabin owned by Allen Mayhew. His wife, Barbara, is a sister of John Kagi, who is one of John Brown's closest associates. Reportedly, the cave under the cabin is reached from a hidden entrance from a nearby ravine."

"Sounds exciting to be so involved in this important work."

"Well, daughter, you are doing important work, too, when you put stitches into this quilt. Now don't be slow and too fancy with your stitchin'. Time is of an essence. We need to get this quilt to Matilda in Jackson County across the river."

"I know. These days are so important to our cause. I'll hurry all I can."

Hiram enters the back door. "What 'er you doin' in there, Sophie? I need you outside to help me pick some rows of corn before that big cloud out there dumps some rain on us."

"I'm just sewin' on a quilt, Hiram!"

"Impatient. Impatient, that's a man fer ya!"

"Shh! Mother, he'll hear you!"

"Oh, bosh, who cares!"

Hiram clanks the long-handled drinking cup against the sides of the water pail in the kitchen and slurps down some big gulps. He wipes his brow with the homespun shirtsleeve on his other arm.

"Sophie, did ya hear me? I've got <u>important</u> work out here to do! This country hasn't been built by pretty work, but by clearing the land and building factories and roads and…"

"Yes, Hiram."

"Yes, Hiram," sarcastically in a whisper.

"Mother, don't aggravate him! Let 'im talk – we know what the real work is."

Hiram stands in the doorway, glaring at Sophie. "What's the matter with you, girl, in here mumbling to yerself! You all right?"

"Yes, Hiram."

"Well, git your buttocks out here and help me! What's so dang important about that quilt your cousin brang across the river anyway…it's jes' pretty work. And your ma's in no hurry for it. She's been dead for months."

"Yes, you're right, Hiram!"

"Don't ya even know what's <u>important</u> anymore?" The screen door slams as he stomps out.

Sophie stabs the needle through the quilt, yanks it tight, knots it, clips it.

"Yes, Hiram, I do!"

Little Lost Girls Of The Bluffs
(Two stories entwined)

"May we go over to that playground, Mama? There's a really cool slipper slide and swing set over there!"

"Yes, Mama, please!" Susan and Shelley implored their mother, who was busy clearing away the remains of their picnic.

"Well, I suppose, but don't go any further. Those woods over there behind the playground look like you could get lost in them."

"We won't, Mama."

"Can we take Ginger with us? She's tired of being in her kennel."

"Yes, our puppy has been shut up in that kennel all the way across Iowa. Can we let her out to play with us and get some exercise?"

"All right, but keep her on the leash so she won't get away!"

"We will! Here, Ginger, let's get you out of here." Soon the girls were racing along the parking lot, blond ponytails swinging in the sunshine. They had stopped at this park near Council Bluffs, Iowa, on the second day of their family vacation. Jeannie smiled to herself as she gazed after her five-year-old twins who raced to the slipper slide. Shelly grasped

Ginger to her breast with one arm as she climbed the steps of the slide. She swooped down with a squeal, holding the little dog tightly in her arms. Susan came down close behind, also with a squeal and a shout. Jeannie's husband, Don, had gone on a walk to stretch his legs after the long hours in the car. Jeannie sighed contentedly here in the sweet fresh air of the park. She stowed the cooler in the trunk and resolved to relax for a few minutes.

My name is Mattie Joseph. I am a Mormon midwife. This is the site here at Kanesville (which was later renamed Council Bluffs) that we set up Winter Quarters where we would live until we resumed our journey to the new Jerusalem in the Great Salt Lake Valley. Brigham Young, our leader, made a treaty to set up a command post here on the banks of the Missouri in 1846.

Since there are so many young families in our settlement, and so many young women having babies, I have often heard, "Sister Joseph, come quickly, my wife's time has come." It's not easy making sure all these babies arrive safely, but using my self-taught skills and experience, and with God's help, I do the best I can.

Jeannie was so engrossed in daydreaming that at first she wasn't aware that she no longer heard the voices of the twins echoing across the ravine. What had it been? Five minutes that she had had her mind on other things…but eons of time when a child just disappears out of sight.

"Susan! Shelley!" she raced to the playground, looked in all directions, her heart dropping to her shoe tops. She looked toward the car and saw Don striding toward her. He had heard her frantic calls for the girls.

"Oh, Don, they are gone! I just took my eyes off them for a few minutes and they are gone!" Jeannie's eyes revealed her fear.

"Relax, Jeannie, they couldn't have gone far this fast. We'll find them!"

> *"Mrs. Joseph, don't despair. I know you did everything you could," the young husband tried to comfort me, he whose grief was a gaping wound. It had been a long and painful delivery, a breech birth from which neither mother or child survived. I stood there with the afterbirth still on my hands and arms, blood soaking my apron. Such agony, such horror on this day in muddy Kanesville.*

"Don, we've got to get help! We've searched for ten minutes, and there's no sign of them. What if – what if someone abducted them? Oh, they could be miles away – and who knows with what kind of pervert!"

"Jeannie, let's not get frantic. Let's try to think clearly here." Don wrapped her in his arms. "We'll call the park rangers and ask for help."

*The trip across Iowa to Winter Quarters had been
a struggle. The weather was terrible and we were
plagued with heavy rains, making travel with the
wagons and livestock extremely slow. When we finally
made it to the "Missouri Bottom," it was a quagmire,
resulting from the heavy rains...what an ordeal with
mud and water up to the axles and miring down the
wheels. Some of the saints were without oxen and
carried all their belongings in a handcart, which they
pulled or pushed. After all the drudgery of walking
hundreds of miles through bad weather, with poor
forage, bad diets, sickness and hunger, death was our
constant companion. We had inadequate provisions
from the beginning and were ill prepared for the trek
west. We had been driven out of many places, Nauvoo,
Illinois, for the last, and persecuted for our religious
beliefs. The attackers took many of our possessions; we
were a poor and desperate band of travelers.*

"I'll go with the rangers. You
stay with the car, Jeannie. If
the girls come back, we'll want
them to find one of us here."

Jeannie nodded numbly. She
dropped to the front seat of
the car, let her head fall on the
steering wheel and convulsed
into shaking sobs. "Why, oh why was I so stupid...why did
I ever take my eyes off them, even for a second. My darling,
laughing daughters. Just last night they romped on the beds
at the motel, having a pillow fight, fresh from their showers,
dressed in their new "princess" nightgowns. They had been
having so much fun on this long awaited vacation...oh, where
are they? God, please take care of them..."

*During our time at Winter Quarters in 1847, we
planted fall crops, rebuilt broken wagons, hunted,
dried meat, rested and worshipped. The men built three
ferries so we could cross the Missouri River in the
spring and head to Zion. But it was a terrible winter
– hundreds died! Malaria, pneumonia and tuberculosis
were illnesses brought on by poor living conditions
and exposure. My best friend and many others died
of scurvy, which came from a lack of "greens" or
vegetables in their diet. One evening I came back to
our rude dwelling to find my husband, Jeb, and our
daughters, two redheaded angels, burning up with fever.
Lily died in my arms that night. Her sister followed her
to heaven on the following day. My hands were useless
against the specter of death. My heart felt as though
it had been ripped from my body. Jeb lived, and we
continued with our westward-bound party in the spring,
but I so despaired of leaving our daughters behind,
there in the cemetery at Kanesville.*

"Jeannie! Jeannie! The rangers have the girls in hand down by
the water hydrant near the equipment shed." Don was running

to her across the grassy expanse of the playground to give her the good news.

"Oh, Don, thank the Lord!" Jeannie dashed from the car and ran to him.

"It seems the dog got away from them and they followed her into the woods."

Tears of joy and relief flooded Jeannie's face as she turned to the beautiful sight of her daughters returning to her. They broke loose from the ranger's hands and ran to their mother, Ginger loping along behind. Jeannie swept each of them up, one in each arm.

"I'm so sorry that I ever let you out of my sight! Oh, thank God, thank God!"

"Mama, why are you so upset?"

"Yes, Mama, you shouldn't cry. There were two little girls who showed us the way back, and they told us not to worry!"

"What little girls?"

"Those little girls with red hair who led us out of the deepest part of the woods!"

Where Jesse James Met His Waterloo

On the corner of 12th and Penn in St. Joseph, Missouri,
stands a little cottage, last home of one of the most notorious
Americans to ever live. His name was Jesse James and he was
shot in the back of the head and killed by one of his own gang
members as he stood on a chair straightening a "Home Sweet
Home" needlework picture which his mother had made. Bob
Ford was the so called "friend" whose name is forever linked
with his renowned prey, as well as the co-conspirator brother,
Charlie Ford, who was also in the room that day.

As one looks toward the western side of this little house, the
windows flicker with an otherworldly light that appears to be
more than the sunset reflection off the Missouri River which is
only a horse's whinny away. Some say this last abode of Jesse
James and his little family is haunted for lights still flicker in
the windows far after dusk, and those who pay to go through
the house often feel a cold shiver as they breathe in the very
air of that place. The bullet hole is now guarded by a plate of
glass to stop prying hands from carrying away souvenirs of the

plaster that surrounded the hole where the bullet that plowed through Jesse's head came to rest.

So who haunts this little house tucked away in the hills of St. Joe in the Missouri River country? Is it the ghost of Jesse who still prowls, planning his next revenge? Or is it the ghost of Robert Ford, a young glory-seeking Judas hoodlum whose greed for the $10,000 reward made him a pariah instead of a hero? Or could the tormented ghost be that of the guilt-ridden Charlie Ford, the brother who committed suicide less than a year after that fateful April 3, 1882, in St. Joe?

And then there is Jesse's wife, Zerelda, the fair young woman, a cousin, who married him when he was twenty-seven, married him knowing he was a hunted outlaw with a bounty on his head. They and their two children lived in many places under assumed names as the Howard family. One wonders what it was like being married to a man who always wore his guns and barely slept at night; always with a gun in his hand, with a gun in his small thin hands that were lightning with a trigger. One wonders if the shining gilt of his Colt and Winchester didn't wear off her attraction for her brash and bold warrior who grew up in the crucible of the border wars on his mother's farm near Kearney, Missouri.

Some people believe that Jesse was a victim of fate and circumstance. He and his older brother, Frank, were the sons of a Baptist preacher who went west to the gold fields to strike it rich and assure the education of his two sons. But he became sick in California and died, never to see his family again. Their mother, also named Zerelda, was a good woman who continued to nurture her sons in Christian ways. Her second marriage ended in divorce when the husband mistreated her sons. Her third marriage was to a kindly Dr. Samuel who championed Frank and Jesse to the bitter end. Three more children were born to Zerelda in her third union. Jesse loved children and was very attached to Archie, the oldest of the stepbrothers, who later met a tragic fate.

Since the James family originated from the South and had Southern loyalties during the Civil War, they were often hounded by the anti-slavery federals after the war. Frank, who was five years older than Jesse, fought for the Confederacy in the War. One day a federal militia came to the Samuel farm, arrested the good doctor and took him to a large tree some distance from the farmhouse. Keeping out of sight, Zerelda followed them. The militia strung Dr. Samuels up by the neck to the branch of a large tree and left him there to die, riding off to find the young Jesse, fifteen at the time, to give him a "lesson."

Meanwhile, Zerelda was able to cut down her husband, who was strangling to death, and breathe life back into him. The posse found Jesse (who looked even younger than his fifteen years) with his hands on a plowshare, working in a distant field. They took a knotted rope and whipped him down the cornrows all the way back to the house.

"We won't hang him this time.
He's too young to fight like that wild devil Frank James, but we'll teach him not to be a Southern sympathizer," they said.

The tears Jesse shed that day were not only for the bloody welts that burned his back, but for the gross lashes to his spirit. Jesse determined to join Quantrill's raiders and serve alongside his brother, Frank. "You're too young, ya whelp," laughed some of the guerrilla force, "go on home to your ma."

Quantrill was one of the fiercest fighters to come out of the Civil War and was a deadly raider in the border wars between Missouri and Kansas. The border warfare lasted two long years and set the land on either side of the Missouri River around Kansas City ablaze. Some proclaim that Jackson County in Missouri at that time was the reddest spot on the map of the United States. Homes and other buildings were set on fire and men were hanged in trees or in their barns. Quantrill and his raiders were upset by the damage the federals did in Osceola, Missouri, and in retribution they planned and carried out the horrendous burning and sacking of Lawrence, Kansas, in 1863.

Even though the teenage Jesse was deemed too young, within the year he and a neighbor, Jim Cummins, who was about Jesse's age, had joined up with the infamous raiders. The boys were under the command of Bloody Bill Anderson, who asserted about Jesse, "For a beardless boy, he is the best fighter in the command."[1]

Thus, Jesse was an apt student of the gun and horse as his manhood was formed by the ruthless men he admired. Friends who rode and fought with the James brothers were the Younger brothers who later became their cohorts in the crimes of holding up banks and robbing trains.

It is widely believed that when Jesse was a youth of eighteen, he was one of the bandits who robbed the Liberty Bank in Clay County, Missouri. Jesse has been reputed to have been a jokester and of a jolly nature as opposed to the serious demeanor of his brother, Frank. While inside the Liberty Bank during the robbery, Greenup Bird, cashier, was ordered to "open the vault and do it quick, or I'll off ya!" Once the vault of stone and brick was opened, the gunslingers helped themselves to the contents. Then one of them said, "All birds should be caged" as he slammed the door on the hapless cashier. This pun was of the joking sort that many attribute to the lips of Jesse James. It also bespeaks that the robber was a local man who knew Bird's name.

The bandits got away with $60,000 in this first-ever daylight robbery. Some of the outlaws were stationed as lookouts as they sat astride their horses in front of the bank. One of the outlaws shot and killed a 19-year-old boy, George Wymore, who was standing on the street across from the bank.

This was the beginning of Jesse's career of robbing and killing which continued until his death at the age of 34. Always so elusive, always able to evade the law, wanted by sheriffs, citizens, marshals and Pinkerton men. How could he simply evaporate into the countryside? Where did he hide? In thickly wooded canyons, in the caves along the Missouri River, in far-off states? Jesse ran scared with a high price on his head for sixteen years! It could never have happened in modern America because of one serious problem the lawmen of old confronted – they didn't know what Jesse James looked like! There were no photos and only sketchy details which came from a few witnesses. This was a terrible hindrance when trying to track down a criminal. Nonetheless, they tried, thousands tried to catch the elusive James brothers.

One young Pinkerton man named Witcher (or Whicher, in some sources) was confident that he could do the job that no one else had accomplished. He was warned by an ex-sheriff, "You'll never catch him. He'll kill you first! I warn you, he'll kill you!"

But Witcher persisted in his plan to disguise himself as an itinerant farmhand and get work on the Samuel's farm. Jesse had a few friends in the area, and one of them heard about the detective's arrival in town and tipped off Jesse. Young Witcher walked down a road near the farm and was stopped by Jesse and a few of his renegades. He asked about Witcher's business, and when the detective said he was simply trying to find work as a field hand, Jesse examined his smooth hands and proclaimed, "You're no farmhand, you're a Pinkerton, that's what you are!"

Witcher denied it for a while, but in the end begged for his life. "Let's not do it here (meaning on the Clay County side of the Missouri River). Let's take him over to Jackson County. " The bandits bound and gagged Witcher, rode to the Blue Mills Ferry and awoke the elderly ferryman at 2:00 a.m., proclaiming they had caught "this horse thief" and needed to get him across the river pronto to find the rest of his gang. The next morning there was a mysterious dead body lying on the road to Blue Mills. J.W.W. was neatly tattooed in the skin above his wrists. Later, it was determined that J.W.W. was one John W. Witcher, lately a Pinkerton man.

This cold-blooded killing may be argued self-defense, but whatever it and all the other killings were, they were an antithesis of who Jesse James was raised to be by his mother. She taught him the Bible and urged him to never say oaths, which he never did in front of women and children. He disliked whiskey and never drank, smoked or chewed. One fellow bandit said that Jesse was loved by all in the camp, that he was gentle and thoughtful.

What about that faithful mother who raised her sons to be devout and honorable men but saw them defiled and corrupted by war? Because of the sins of her sons, she suffered tremendously. Once a band of Pinkertons, bent on destroying the James brothers (who, on this particular night, had already slipped away) threw a firebomb through the window of her home, mangling her arm and killing eight-year-old Archie. Her forearm had to be amputated. According to Robertus Love (a man who chronicled this chapter in history and who knew Zerelda James personally in later years), she was "a woman of infinite sorrows, of well-nigh infinite capacity for suffering. She was a strong woman – in body, in mind, in soul – she was a woman thoroughly good and noble – the one wholly heroic character in the whole unhappy outfit."[2]

So, is it the mother who lights windows in the little house where her handiwork was so lovingly hung by her star-crossed son? Does her ghost yet hover in these little rooms, mourning her long-lost son?

Or are the ghosts who inhabit this house, the ones of the Pinkerton man Witcher, or the cashiers, conductors, engineers and innocent citizens who died at the hand of the infamous outlaw. Do their spirits surge yet to damn the soul of the one who lived in this house and robbed them of their earthly lives.

Whoever they are..one thing is certain, the ghost of Jesse James rides on through legend, song, ode and story. His image has been projected onto the silver screen, portrayed by dozens upon dozens of actors. Jesse James cannot escape the handcuffs of his own legacy. He lives on, a gallant warrior turned treacherous, cold-blooded killer, a man whose name is as well known as any in American history. A name more recognized abroad than many of our statesmen and presidents.

He was a sweet little farm boy from the Missouri River country who became embroiled in a violent lifestyle that haunted him to the grave.

[1] Love, Robertus, <u>The Rise and Fall of Jesse James</u>, Bison Books, University of Nebraska Press, 1990, pg. 47

[2] IBID, pg. 155

Ghost Wife Of The Sioux

One of the most handsome and brave of the Sioux warriors was Thunder Cloud. All of the tribe that resided with him along the banks of the Missouri River near Yankton, South Dakota, revered him, and all the young maidens vied to serve him around the tribal fire. The braves were never afraid to ride with him for they knew his prowess with the arrow and the horse, and they knew they could count on him in any situation in battle or when on the hunt.

One summer day, the braves had just returned from an especially successful buffalo expedition. There was much celebration in camp, and Thunder Cloud, as the leader, was gravely thanked by the Sioux Chief. As a reward, the Chief offered his daughter, Little Red Wing, to the dauntless warrior.

Thunder Cloud had long noticed the shy and lovely Red Wing and was happy to accept the Chief's daughter as his wife. She joined Thunder Cloud in his tepee and the couple dwelt in a state of bliss for many moons there by the banks of the wide

Missouri. Whenever Thunder Cloud came back from one of his forays, Red Wing rushed into his arms. She adored this handsome hero of her people, and was overjoyed when she gave birth to a boy within the year. Little Running Bear was the darling of the Sioux and the pride of his grandfather, the Chief.

Within another year Running Bear was joined by another papoose, and the little family thrived. But the third time Red Wing became pregnant, things did not go so well. Despite all the best efforts of the old squaws and the Medicine Man, the child was too large to be delivered. Red Wing and her third son died.

Thunder Cloud was heartbroken. He helped to rope her lifeless form onto a travois to be pulled by a pony to the burial grounds. Once there, the pallet was hoisted high on stakes to preserve the body from wandering wolves. A sad procession attended the burial and then wound its way back to camp.

The Indians mourned the passing of the lovely Red Wing, but none as deeply as Thunder Cloud. After many hours of fasting and despair, he forded the Missouri River where it was most shallow and rode his horse to the highest bluff on the opposite side. There on the sage and rocks of Holy Ground, he threw himself prostrate on the ground and yearned for one more touch from the gentle hand of Red Wing.

After several days of lying there almost comatose from dehydration and agony, he heard someone call his name: "Thunder Cloud. Thunder Cloud, it is me." And wonder of wonders, it was the sweet voice of his beloved. He raised his head slowly to see her walking toward him along the ridge of the bluff.

Thunder Cloud was overjoyed! Red Wing held out a leather pouch of water and her dazed husband drank from it. "Have you come back from the Spirit World in the flesh, or are you a ghost?" he asked, still somewhat in a stupor.

"I am not of flesh like you," Red Wing answered, "but you, in your great distress, have called my spirit back. I have been given power from the West Wind for two different intentions, my dearest Thunder Cloud. You must make the choice."

"What are the choices?" he asked, still blinking in disbelief at the lovely apparition before him.

"Either you and our children can join me in the Spirit World, or I will come back to the Earth World on one condition."

"Oh, I could not yet leave the pleasure of hunting buffalo and riding my pony over the plains, please come back to dwell with me on Mother Earth."

"I will do that on one condition. Will you always be true to me until we both shall enter the Happy Hunting Grounds together?"

Thunder Cloud rose up from the ground and clasped Red Wing into his arms. "Yes, forever and always," he breathed into her ear.

So the young couple left the Sacred Grounds. Hand in hand, they walked once again into their tribal camp. The Sioux stood in awe to see Red Wing once again, and murmurings spread like wildfire through the camp. Is it really her, or is it someone who looks like her? Some of the old squaws were sure she was a ghost, cackling behind her back and giving her wide berth.

Red Wing clasped her two small children to her heart and barely let them out of her sight. Thunder Cloud beamed with delight upon his little brood. The family was once again together and love flowed as generously from their hearts as the rolling waters flowed within the banks of the wide Missouri.

The earth revolved through sunrises and sunsets, through the warm seasons and through the cold seasons. Time tends to change things, takes a toll of its own. Red Wing's face became leathery in the sun and wind. Thunder Cloud started noticing a striking young maiden called "Laughing Water." He determined to take her as a second wife.

Red Wing bore this humiliation and betrayal for a while, but his visits to her tent became more and more infrequent. He spent more time with the doe-eyed Laughing Water in his second tepee.

Then one day as the squaws were preparing hides for the winter, Red Wing overheard Laughing Water bragging about how much more attention she got than Thunder Cloud's first wife.

"He has broken his promise," Red Wing whispered to herself as the tears streamed down her face. "He has broken his promise and I can no longer ignore it. I will claim what is mine!"

That night Red Wing, the ghost wife, took her children and her husband and went back to the Spirit World, leaving Laughing Water crying there on the banks of the wide Missouri.

A Letter From Lewis To Clark

Dear Clark, my trusted friend and comrade,

I must relate to you the truth about my demise. What a travesty that I should travel with you and the Corps of Discovery over 7,689 miles, escaping from so many dangers, and then be overcome by the savagery of politics. I know you have heard it said that I committed suicide four years after returning from our historic journey up the Missouri River, across the mountains and down the Columbia River and arriving at the Pacific Ocean! What an historic odyssey it was! And I survived during those two years and four months when the odds were against it, and came to the pitiful end of being murdered by political enemies.

Some "witnesses" reported that I was depressed and drinking heavily. Those witnesses were political rivals and therefore, unreliable. One was General James Wilkinson, my predecessor as governor of the Louisiana Territory, and another was Major Neely, who was closely allied with General Wilkinson. The major was accompanying me on my journey to Washington,

D.C., to clear my name on some matters. On the night of my death at Mrs. Grinder's roadhouse in Tennessee, Major Neely had disappeared for a few hours. Did that not seem strange to the investigators?

And that woman, Mrs. Grinder…for two hours after she heard the gunshots, she would not come out of her room to aid me! I begged her to help me, to get me some water, but she would not come out. Don't they realize it was a political conspiracy and even the Grinders were in on it? If I were going to commit suicide, I wouldn't need two shots – one in my side and one in my head! As an expert huntsman, I could have made one shot do the deed.

Yes, I did whisper the words "so hard to die" as I lay on that bloody pallet, but that is not my ghost that some claim to hear in the wind near my gravesite saying "so hard to die" and that is not me who scrapes the water dipper against the bottom of an empty bucket. These are the sounds invented by the parties involved – it is their guilt that haunts them.

Ah, my dear friend and comrade, if anyone knows where my ghost roams, it is you. My spirit traverses again all those miles of the mighty Missouri River, riding high on the crest of the current, experiencing again that amazing journey.

How honored I was when President Jefferson chose me in 1804 to lead an exploration into the uncharted regions of the Louisiana Purchase. And how doubly honored that you consented to be my co-helmsman.

Oh, yes, we had many difficult circumstances, including grizzly bears, rattlesnakes, hunger and extremely cold winters. Do you remember that winter we spent camped on the Missouri River in South Dakota near the Mandans when the temperature dipped to 40 degrees below zero? Our moccasins froze stiff as boards, as well as the ink in my pen. Remember that Mandan Indian who was out in the cold all night (it was about 30 below) and he came back the next morning unfazed. How hardy those Mandans were! Wasn't it spectacular watching them jump from ice floe to ice floe, some patches barely a foot in diameter, as they chased the buffalo?

It was at the Mandan camp that we met Charbonneau, the fur trader who lived among them with his teenage wife, Sacagawea. What unbelievably good fortune that she joined us with her husband as a translator and guide, and as a liaison to the Indian tribes. How joyful she was when we met the Shoshoni Indians, her people from whom she had been kidnapped by the Hidatsu Indians as a child, and discovered the Shoshoni chief was her own brother! Her influence helped us get the much-needed horses from her tribe.

It was amazing that
we were able to strike
up good relations with
most of the Indians in
our travels, especially
important were the
beads and medallions
we brought as peace
offerings. I have
to exclude those
Blackfeet for they
were vicious, and
more fitting that I should have been killed in my battle with
them on the trip back from the ocean when they were trying
to steal our guns and horses as we lay near our campfire. I had
to kill two of them. Ironically, it was the so-called "civilized"
white men who actually did me in.

Another time I most certainly could have perished on our
journey was when Cruzatte, of our own party, mistook me
for an elk and shot me in the hind side. He was blind in one
eye and nearsighted in the other, so I could far sooner forgive
him than the black hearts who took deliberate aim at me at the
Grinder house.

If I were to die, wouldn't it have been more tolerable if it had
been from that wound by Cruzatte. True, it was painful and I
lay on my belly on the floor of the boat for many days, unable
even to keep my log, but I survived.

We were so often hungry, and at times even had to butcher one
of our horses. Remember the Christmas on the coast when we
ate rotten elk meat and roots, but we celebrated with fortitude.
We survived by our wits, with our imagination and with good
humor.

We were a hardy crew. Future generations will continue to enjoy reading our journals and maps, our descriptions of plants and animals that we scouted out all along the uncharted miles on that brown coursing artery through the heart of America, the grand Missouri River.

That river could easily have sunk our keelboats, pirogues and canoes, but it spared us, even from the Great Falls in Montana that caused us so much trouble.

Our names, Meriwether Lewis and William Clark, are engraved on monuments all along the course of the Missouri River. Our names will forever be linked with that of the Missouri.

Some say that my ghost wails near my grave in Tennessee. Hogwash! My spirit rides the flowing currents of OUR river and at night I lie under the stars on her banks, just as we did so many years ago. Ah! Those were the days, my friend.

With sincerity and gratitude,
Lewis

Strong Man Of The Half-Breeds

In the southeast corner of Nebraska in the Barada Hills lived one of the strongest men of American folklore. His name was Antoine Barada and he was born to a Frenchman named Michael Barada and his Indian bride, Tae-Gle-Ha, or, as she was also known, Laughing Buffalo. Their romance was the stuff of fairy tales. Supposedly, she had dropped a red rose to Michael from a window in France when she was visiting there with a special delegation from the New World.

The nobleman looked up and swooned, such a beautiful maiden was she. The next day he went to the house where she had been seen and inquired for her. But he was too late – she had sailed for America that very day. He followed her to America and searched the length and breadth of the frontier, always asking if anyone knew Tae-Gle-Ha, his Laughing Buffalo. After several years he found her living among her native Omaha tribe, and she, too, had never married, perhaps waiting for the handsome nobleman. Very soon they were married. A big, strong half-breed boy was born to them in 1807 and they named him Antoine.

When Antoine was only seven years old, it is written that a band of Sioux rode by one day. They cackled and pointed at the awesome size of the child, snatched him up and thundered off over the prairies with their god-like prize.

Months later, fur traders spotted Antoine and paid the ransom of two ponies which the Sioux demanded. During the time that Antoine rode with the Northwestern Fur Company, a lifelong passion for hunting was stirred in him. The bluffs of the Missouri River were rich with bountiful game, and he became an expert trapper and hunter.

Finally, the fur traders delivered Antoine back to his home at Fort Lisa. Michael Barada gladly reimbursed the traders two ponies for their efforts. Determined to keep their son safe from further attacks, the parents sent him east to enroll in a military school. However, his escorts were a reckless soldier pack.

The soldiers got drunk and lost their charge near St. Louis where an aunt, Mme. Mousette, took him in and taught him to read and write. She found him to be an amazing child possessing both brawn and wit.

In his aunt's town of Carondolet, south of St. Louis, Antoine became renowned for his athletic feats. His muscles rippled as he tossed a 1500-pound barrel of flour in the air. Everyone was awed by this strong young man with the high cheekbones and the flashing black hair.

In his later teens, Antoine left Carondolet and went north to work in quarries, tossing stone. It is here that one of his greatest feats occurred. According to witnesses, Antoine hefted a boulder weighing <u>eighteen hundred pounds</u> and placed it as a doorsill for the arsenal, and he did it all alone. Bystanders gasped at this Herculean feat – never had they seen a young man so strong! They swear the doorsill remained there for many years, and the mighty act was registered in military records as proof.

When Antoine was twenty-five, he crossed the state of Missouri to visit his parents who were living among the Omaha tribe. For a while he worked as a scout, leading parties of adventurers over the mountains.

As he traveled, his heart pined for a fair young woman named Josephine whom he had left behind in Missouri. So he turned his horse's head around and galloped off to St. Louis to fulfill his dream. He and Josephine were married there in 1836 with parents and friends as witnesses.

Seven children were born to this union and 'Toine (as he was affectionately known) supported them with his useful skill of trapping and selling fur.

After many years, he became restless when he heard the cry of "Gold!" echoing from the western coast. His adventuring spirit ran strong and so Barada joined the California Gold Rush of '49.

If one of the westward covered wagons got stuck in the mud, 'Toine would come and simply lift it out to the cheers of his traveling companions. They also knew that if they were hungry, 'Toine would find game without fail. The tales of his prowess grew all along the overland trail.

His popularity wasn't only because he was strong, but he was affable and fun to be with. He was always willing to lend a hand, sunny and good-natured. No wonder he was loved by all who came to know him on the westward trek.

Antoine didn't strike the mother lode while in the gold fields. However, he did find enough gold to fashion some earrings for his dear Josephine, which she proudly wore until her death.

After six years in California, he came back to his native hunting grounds, visited his mother's Omaha tribe in the bluffs of Nebraska, and decided to settle down.

He claimed a farm in Richardson County, 'mid rolling hills on a half-breed tract (a parcel of land designated by the government for half-breed use). He was known among his neighbors for his kind ways and generous acts.

He was also known as a "hurry up" kind of man, always rushing about. One day he got "riled up" at a pole driver who was delaying a boat that was idling on the Missouri River, waiting to be tied up. 'Toine got so exasperated that he picked up the hammer, derrick and maul and threw them all the way across the river into Iowa. At least, that's what the legends say.

Then he pounded the pole down into the ground with his bare fist. Folk tales say that he hit an artesian well which spouted water fifty feet or more into the air! But probably that's a bit of an exaggeration.

Others say that when farmers brought loads of hogs to old St. DeRoin town on the river, they put Antoine in charge of tossing each hog upon the southbound barge. Oh, the grunting and squealing racket that was raised as Antoine threw those porkers onto the flat boats below.

'Toine was an excellent marksman who shot prairie chickens on the fly. Once he killed a bear which had treed a man. The man was in such shock that he couldn't come down even after the bear was shot, so Antoine kindly climbed the tree and carried the fellow to camp upon his back.

When picnics were held in the Barada Hills, settlers from miles around came to join in the fun. They feasted on wild turkey, venison and buffalo, and later competed in games such as long jumping and horseshoe pitching. Of course, Antoine was always champion and held every record.

But people didn't mind, for Antoine was so friendly and down-to-earth with a wonderful sense of humor. His presence was desired at every community event.

By 1881, the big man was plumb worn out from 75 years of an action-packed life, and on March 30, he departed for the "happy hunting grounds." A tall gravestone stands west of the village of Barada as evidence of his passing.

But strange things still happen around Barada. For instance, there was the terrible tornado in the early 1900s. A roof was torn off Klepper's big barn – just lifted up and set down in a neighboring alfalfa field. The next morning, lo and behold, the roof had been neatly replaced atop the barn's walls. Who could have performed such a strong and kindly deed?

Once Jarvis' wagonload of corn lost a wheel. He walked to get help and when he came back, the wheel had been replaced under the wagon and bolted to the axle. Who was responsible for such a marvelous deed?

Those in the hills and hollows of Barada can attest to other strongman feats still happening to this day that could only have been executed by the ghost of a legendary man with a big, big heart…Antoine Barada.

The Oldest Halloween Parade

It was Halloween in Hiawatha, Kansas, in 1913. The children of the town were especially full of pranks and tricks that year. In fact, they were running wild! They chased each other through the yards, trampling the flowerbeds. They pulled the cats by their tails and threw them into rain barrels. Some of the children had ponies which they galloped through the gardens. Pumpkins and tomatoes were squashed under the hooves of the horses.

A few of the bigger boys pushed over outhouses. "Let's play a trick on Mr. Milligan," they tittered. "When he comes out of his house to use the 'john,' let's lift it up and carry him into the street."

Sure enough, Mr. Milligan came out and the ornery boys converged on the toilet. "One! Two! Three!" they said. Then they all heaved together on "three" and lifted the little building into the air with Mr. Milligan seated on the one-holder inside. They carried the outhouse and all into the middle of the street and set it down.

Mr. Milligan emerged, huffing and puffing in anger, pulling up his overalls and shaking his fist at the boys who were hiding in the bushes and snorting with laughter.

Mrs. Krebs stood on her porch and saw the whole thing. "Oh dear, these pranks are getting out of hand," she declared.

She surveyed her mashed marigolds and mangled hydrangea bushes. She saw the mess of smashed pumpkins on the sidewalks and in the alley, and she wondered what she could do to give the children (and the adults) a better Halloween.

"I know!" she said as a light bulb went on in her head. "I'll host a party – a frolic – next year! That will give the young people something to do instead of getting into trouble."

The next September she sent out invitations to all the children in her part of town. They read:

> Please come to my house in costume on October 31. Decorate your trikes and wagons. Treats will be served. Signed: Mrs. John Krebs.

The children were excited. The parents were delighted, and Mr. Milligan heaved a sigh of relief. There were no two ways about it, Mrs. Krebs had saved the flower gardens this year, and made it safer for all outhouses users.

Word got around. The next year, 1915, was an even larger success. More children from more neighborhoods were invited. "What shall I wear this year to the frolic at Mrs. Krebs' house?" was the question of every child in town.

Treadle sewing machines were humming as mothers sewed up princess gowns, witch dresses and cowboy suits. Some of the children merely took old sheets, cut out holes for eyes and nose and went as ghosts. Some were hobos and some were scarecrows.

Everyone enjoyed Halloween so much in 1915 that even bigger plans were made for the following year. There would be a parade <u>and</u> a pet contest. There was an article in the town newspaper after the event which read:

> The second annual Halloween frolic sponsored by Mrs. Krebs was well attended. Folks lined Oregon Street sidewalks to enjoy the children's parade. Some adults also dressed up and partook in the revelry. Tricks and pranks were again at a minimum this year. The community is indebted to Mrs. Krebs.

The frolic gained in popularity year after year. People in the rural areas and smaller towns around also became involved. Out in the country west of Hiawatha in 1925, there lived a farmer with his wife and nine children. They had heard such great things about the Halloween events and decided to attend.

But first, Mr. Hillerton and his children had to milk their twenty-one Holsteins.

"Hurry up!" yelled Billy Joe to little Jerry as they brought up the cows from the pasture. "The parade starts at 8:00 and we have to drive twenty miles in our old rickety truck."

"Get along!" shouted Jerry as he headed a pokey cow toward the barn. The boys could hardly wait to see the famous Hiawatha parade.

In the house, Mrs. Hillerton directed the older girls to wash the faces of the younger children. "Lilly Ann, be sure that their dresses and overalls are clean."

"Yes, Mama," said Lilly Ann as she scurried about. Oh, why did they have to be late to everything because of the milking chores!

Lilly Ann brushed and slicked down the straw-like hair of the twins, Howie and Brucie. She quickly braided Lulu's long pigtails.

At last the cows were milked and the family climbed aboard the old farm truck. The children sat on wooden benches in the back of the truck. At the last minute, Mr. Hillerton loaded on several bushels of apples they had picked from their trees that day. Maybe they could sell them to Mr. Shelton, the grocer, after the parade.

"Hold on!" called back Dad Hillerton as he put the truck into reverse. It bucked a bit, but soon the family was on its way over some bumpy country roads to Hiawatha.

"Hurry, Daddy!" hollered Billy Joe. "We don't want to be late!"

The Hillertons arrived in town well after eight o'clock and found the streets crowded with Model T cars, horses, carriages and the town square full of people. There was no place to park and no way to see the parade!

"I have an idea! Let's just enter the parade," grinned Dad to Mother Hillerton. He roared the old truck down a back street, came to the assembly point, and just as the last band and last horses entered the parade route, Mr. Hillerton yelled to his kids, "Hold on, we'll just bring up the rear of the parade. If we can't see it, by golly, we'll be in it!"

"Oh, Daddy, how embarrassing," moaned Lilly Ann as she buried her head in her hands and sank lower on her seat. But Billy Joe and the boys hallooed their agreement to this outrageous plan. They shouted and waved at the crowd as the noisy old truck jolted along the parade route. The bystanders laughed and pointed at the funny backwoods family. Billy Joe picked up an apple and threw it to a little goblin. Others shouted for apples, too, and the boys bombarded them into the crowd to the amusement of all.

"How mortifying!" said Lilly Ann, who scooched down even lower as apples went zinging past her head. She wondered if she would ever outlive the humiliation of this night.

But as a senior in high school, Lilly Ann was selected to be one of the queen candidates from the surrounding small towns. On a crisp evening, she sat in her formal gown on the royalty float, shivering and throwing kisses to the crowd. How much better to be throwing kisses instead of apples!

Fifteen years after that, in 1945, Billy Joe drove the yellow Minneapolis Moline tractor that pulled a float bearing Mrs. Krebs as the founder and Grand Marshal of the parade. Lilly Ann brought her husband and children from Denver and joined with others in clapping and cheering for the remarkable lady who had begun a great tradition.

For years after Mrs. Krebs' death, a car with a huge wreath in the backseat was entered into the parade to pay her tribute.

Lilly Ann missed out on the Halloween Frolic for quite a few years after that. Her children grew up and left home. Her husband died. One October, Lilly Ann felt a strong compulsion to go back to Hiawatha and stand under the flaming maple trees along the cobblestone streets to take in the famous Halloween parade. So her youngest son, Seth, and his little boy drove her across the breadth of Kansas so she could recapture some of those special moments. As they watched the parade go down the street, little Sam started laughing as the royalty float went by, for he claimed to see a funny lady wearing a fur coat and a hat with a tall feather on it (exactly the outfit Mrs. Krebs always wore in her parade appearances).

"Look at that old lady! Doesn't she look funny riding on that float with all those girls!" he said, jerking Lilly Ann's hand and pointing toward the float carrying the queen and her attendants.

"Shh! Sammy. I don't see anyone but teenagers on that float."

"Ahem," said a gentleman from behind them. "Ma'am, he probably saw Mrs. Krebs. Her ghost always rides or walks somewhere in the parade. She never misses a one. She just loves this frolic that she founded so many years ago. Many times it's only the young, or the young-at-heart who see her."

Lilly Ann nodded her head, and joined Sammy in waving at the royalty float heading west on Oregon Street.

The Frantic Horsewoman

The sleet began swirling around Jeb and his horse as he clopped down the gravel road west of Yankton. He had hoped he could make it to his uncle's farm on the other side of the Missouri River before nightfall, but the Arctic blast was descending rapidly upon them. Finding shelter from the freezing winds filled with blinding ice crystals was becoming more urgent by the minute. His eyes searched for an old barn, an abandoned farmhouse, anything to get out of the storm!

The dark outline of a building lay up ahead. He turned his horse in that direction and felt his way to a heavy old wooden door. He lifted the latch and found himself in a deserted country schoolhouse. "Come on, Ginger, git in here with me," he commanded, gently tugging on the reins and pulling her over the threshold.

As the man and horse stood in the cloakroom of the old creaking building, howling noises emanated from the inner schoolroom itself. It was a different kind of howling than from a wind-driven storm. It was more a cross between a howl and

a moan and had an eerie human quality.

Ginger's withers quivered nervously and Jeb tried to soothe her, though he himself felt very fidgety. Ginger whinnied softly and buried her nose against Jeb's woolen parka. Jeb peered out the door after many uncomfortable minutes and chose to go out rather than remain here any longer. "Let's git outta this spooky place, old girl," he said as he mounted his horse and prepared to ride out. Thankfully, the main fury of the storm had passed over, but a fine snow was still coming down.

Just as the horse stepped out onto the old stone slab of the schoolhouse, something seemed to fly out behind them and land on the bare rump behind Jeb's saddle.

And the moaning was now right behind his ear! Ginger bolted and reared, causing Jeb to grab the saddle horn. "Whoa! Whoa! Settle down, girl, what's the matter anyway?"

The horse tore off toward the gravel road and kept picking up speed, as if some being was kicking her in the flanks, urging her to go ever faster and faster.

Jeb drew a deep breath and turned enough to see out of the corner of his eye an apparition behind him on the horse. She had long black hair, singed and raggedy looking. Her eyes were huge and filled with a look of horror. She was nearly naked except for a few fluttering strips of what must have been a long dress. Her face and body were scorched black, and the smell of fire and death gagged Jeb as he tried to manage his runaway horse. Some other force was controlling Ginger and frantically pushing her to hurry, hurry on.

The frightened horse attempted to jump a low fence, lost her footing and pitched Jeb headfirst into a snow bank, as she herself fell. Jeb righted himself quickly and looked through the thinly falling snow, but the frantic rider was gone…had simply evaporated into the gauzy dusk.

Luckily, neither Jeb nor his horse was badly hurt, and Jeb was able to find a farm where they were given shelter in a barn.

Jeb asked Mr. Schweizer, the farmer, if he knew anything about the schoolhouse yonder about two miles.

"That's the District 31 school, but it was abandoned and our neighboring children attend the consolidated school over at Kingsburg. You know, that school has quite a history…it burned down in January 1888. But it was rebuilt by the patrons of the district and used until 1940."

"Why did it burn?"

"Haven't you heard what happened in 1888? You must be new in the Midwest. That was the year of the terrible blizzard that killed so many people on the plains – from North Dakota and Montana down through South Dakota and Nebraska."

"Yeah, I did hear somethin' about it…it's called the 'children's blizzard,' isn't it? Because so many schoolchildren were frozen to death on their way home from school."

"Yep, my grandmother told me it was the worst disaster she could ever remember on the prairies, and there were plenty with grasshoppers, drought, hunger and such, but this blizzard just beat all. It is said that on January 12, 1888, the day started out so mild that children went to school without coats and gloves. Farmers went to far fields and on errands on this warm day without nearly enough protection for the cold front that came roarin' down upon 'em. It was so sad finding  the bodies later, includin' little children with their faces frozen to the ground."

"But the schoolhouse fire – what did that have to do with the blizzard?"

"Well, Miss Clara – that was the schoolmarm's name – must have kept her charges at school rather than let them go out into the blinding snow. She musta thought they would be safer there. Some schoolmarms sent their children home and some elected to keep them inside until the storm was over, even if they had to stay there all night. Well, it's figured that Miss Clara musta built up a large fire in the old stove, throwing in lots of hay to keep her burning good. Some people figure the flames musta got out in the stovepipe near the roof and caught it on fire. What a terrible inferno that musta been and how awful for Miss Clara who helplessly watched as the place became enveloped in smoke and flames!"

"That explains the ghost who scared my horse and me half to death! It was a woman, all scorched and horror-stricken who jumped on my horse and spurred it on, like she was frantic to ride for help or somethin'."

"That does, indeed, sound like Miss Clara. Lots of people won't go near the District 31 schoolhouse because they say it's haunted, and because they just can't stand hearin' the sad moanin' that comes outta that building!"

The Ghost Of Paradise Cavern

What a frightening way to wake up. I was asleep in my cabin when I felt a hand rubbed across my face. It was a gloved hand that rested across my mouth. I could hardly breathe, both because of the hand and because it liked to scare the daylights outta me!

And, Cousin Dora, the intruder, had a black neckerchief up over his nose which muffled his fierce warning:

"Wake up, Old Granny, an' tell me where Billy is or I'll jes smother you to death!"

"Mmmrp, glub." I struggled to speak, but it was kinda hard with that hand blockin' out my voice, an' my heart beatin' so hard it was about to jump out of my nightgown.

"Okay. I'll take my hand away. But you tell me where Billy went with that gunnysack of gold nuggets or you won't be alive come sundown!"

It was slowly dawning on me who this varmint must be…he was the drifter my grandson had met in the mountains and together they had filed a claim up in Alder Gulch, up around Virginia City somewhere. This was his partner, Elias Parks.

"C'mon. I don't have all day. Where's Billy? An' where did he hide those nuggets? Some guys at the gulch tol' me all about his big lode find and about his gunnysack! Yore grandson is a two-timin' little thief!"

Billy had stopped by several days ago. He allowed that he

was headin' north toward the caverns near Three Forks, you know, where the Jefferson, Madison and Gallatin Rivers meet up with each other, just six miles from the headwaters of the Missouri River. Billy tol' me Elias an' he had a fallin' out, and Elias took what few nuggets they had at the time and rode off toward Helena to use it up on broads an' loose livin'. While Elias was gone, Billy was a pickin' and a pannin' for all his worth and he had nigh on a thousan' dollars in gold rocks. He tol' me he was aimin' to hide it from Elias, I'll not deny it.

"Speak up, ol' woman. Where's Billy?"

"There's no need to keep blabberin' through that neckerchief. I know you mus' be Elias," I said.

He ripped down the mask. His eyes were hard as flint and I knew he wore deadly serious.

"Iffin' you kill me, then you won't have any idea where he went, will you? You're better off to keep me alive."

He seemed to realize I had a point, so he said, "Alright! Alright! Shoot it to me…where'd he go?"

"Well, I'm not rightly sure. He stopped by here with a sack and all's I know is he was headin' north. Said somethin' about 'Elias could look from Paradise to hell an' back an' he was never gonna get his hands on that sack o' gold!'"

I was wishin' I could get on my mackinaw for the fire was out an' I was shiverin' from the cold.

Elias jes set himself down in my ol' rocker and he jes kept a rockin' an' a rockin'. Then suddenly he jumped up and said, "I've got it, the Caverns! He was goin' to that there cave up there! Git yore shoes and coat on, ol' lady, yore comin' with me!"

"Can't I jes stay here an' make you a delicious stew for when ya come ridin' back?"

"Nonsense! Yore goin' with me, an' iffen we don't find darlin' grandson, I'll take thet gold outta yer hide."

It was early mornin' and still dark when he tied up my hands and threw me astraddle his horse. He climbed into the saddle behind me and, with the horse carefully pickin' his way down the mountainside, we rode toward the caverns.

Late that night, he reined his poor tired horse to a stop outside that queen of all caverns, the Paradise room. I'd heard about those famous caves hollowed out of the limestone by water dripping down through the insides of the mountains for eons of years. I'd heard they were mighty purty, with columns and rock falls and such, but I'd sure rather have visited them under a better set of circumstances!

Elias had a lantern he stole from a campsite nearby the caverns an' he lit it. "Okay, ol' lady, you're comin' with me. You may jes have a recollection an' be able to tell me some more hints about where them nuggets may be!"

'Twas cold and eerie down in them tunnels, let me tell ya, an' I was settin' my boots down carefully every step 'cause we were walkin' along edges of fall-offs where ya didn't dare slip, especially 'cause my hands were still bound up an' it would have been nigh impossible for them to be of any use had I started to fallin'.

After about twenty or thirty minutes or so, Elias flashed the lantern around and spotted a huge stone column that seemed to have a crevice and crawlspace behind it. An old felt hat was lyin' nearby.

"That's ol' Billy's!" his booming voice echoed from wall to wall in that dark chamber. "Looks like ol' Billy may have slipped down into that huge crevice after stashing the gold behind thet big column." Elias threw a rock into it and we never heard it hit bottom.

"Look's like ol' Billy may have fallen into the devil's mouth!" he cackled with glee.

I jes stood there shakin'. "Poor Billy," I thought to myself, "he was a good boy at heart, jes took up with the wrong crowd." I was hopin' thet he hadn't slipped, an' I was prayin' that I wouldn't, when in the dim light, a black ghostlike figure came from behind me, passed right through me, causing the hair on the back of my neck to stand on end. The black apparition startled Elias, who dropped the lantern and started backin' up.

"Billy!" he screamed. His foot slipped on some rocks and he dropped like a snake from a tree. All's I heard were his blood curdlin' screams as he fell into the pit. And that, Cousin Dora, is how I survived.

Dora responded, "But there's more. How did you get out of the cavern, with your hands tied up and all?"

"Well, I picked up the lantern between the two tied-up hands, an' I edged my way, inch by inch, back out the way we had come, retracing our steps the best I could. When I got outside, I took the lantern back to the campsite from where Elias had stolen it. There was a goodly woman there who took pity on me, cut my hands loose and fed me. She offered thet her man would be back soon, an' he would take me home. I allowed that would be right nice, but I'd jes go back to the caverns where Elias' horse was still tied up and ride meself back through the mountains to my cabin.

"You're 'about the strongest granny I've ever known," said Dora. "How about it…are ya goin' back an' get the gold for yourself? You might as well have it, ya know!"

"Shucks, no! What do I need with a sack of gold! I've got my little log cabin and the sun comin' up in the fresh pine-sweet mornin', an' I've got whole blankets of the prettiest little flowers, an' fresh spring water. I've got ol' Bossy who's needin' a good milkin' right about now. I've got my quilts to sew and wild berry jams to make. An' I have a friend like you. What do I need of gold? I have all the Paradise I need right here in the mountains of Montana."

GHOSTS OF INTERSTATE 90 Chicago to Boston by D. Latham

GHOSTS of the *Whitewater Valley* by Chuck Grimes

GHOSTS of Interstate 74   by B. Carlson

GHOSTS of the Ohio Lakeshore Counties   by Karen Waltemire

GHOSTS of *Interstate 65*   by Joanna Foreman

GHOSTS of Interstate 25 by Bruce Carlson

GHOSTS of the Smoky Mountains by Larry Hillhouse

GHOSTS of the Illinois Canal System by David Youngquist

GHOSTS of the *Niagara River* by Bruce Carlson

Ghosts of Little Bavaria   by Kishe Wallace

Shown above (at 85% of actual size) are the spines of other Quixote Press books of ghost stories.
These are available at the retailer from whom this book was procured, or from our office at 1-800-571-2665 cost is $9.95 + $3.50 S/H.

GHOSTS of Lookout Mountain by Larry Hillhouse

GHOSTS of Interstate 77 by Bruce Carlson

GHOSTS of Interstate 94 by B. Carlson

GHOSTS of MICHIGAN'S U. P. by Chris Shanley-Dillman

GHOSTS of the FOX RIVER VALLEY by D. Latham

GHOSTS ALONG I-35 by B. Carlson

Ghostly Tales of Lake Huron by Roger H. Meyer

Ghost Stories by Kids, for Kids by some really great fifth graders

Ghosts of Door County Wisconsin by Geri Rider

Ghosts of the Ozarks B Carlson

Ghosts of US - 63 by Bruce Carlson

Ghostly Tales of Lake Erie by Jo Lela Pope Kimber

GHOSTS OF DALLAS COUNTY	by Lori Pielak
Ghosts of US - 66 from Chicgo to Oklahoma	By McCarty & Wilson
Ghosts of the Appalachian Trail	by Dr. Tirstan Perry
Ghosts of I- 70	by B. Carlson
Ghosts of the Thousand Islands	by Larry Hillhouse
Ghosts of US - 23 in Michigan	by B. Carlson
Ghosts of Lake Superior	by Enid Cleaves
GHOSTS OF THE IOWA GREAT LAKES	by Bruce Carlson
Ghosts of the Amana Colonies	by Lori Erickson
Ghosts of Lee County, Iowa	by Bruce Carlson
The Best of the Mississippi River Ghosts	by Bruce Carlson
Ghosts of Polk County Iowa	by Tom Welch

Ghosts of Interstate 75   by Bruce Carlson

Ghosts of Lake Michigan   by Ophelia Julien

Ghosts of I-10   by C. J. Mouser

GHOSTS OF INTERSTATE 55   by Bruce Carlson

Ghosts of US - 13, Wisconsin Dells to Superior   by Bruce Carlson

Ghosts of I-80   David youngquist

Ghosts of Interstate 95   by Bruce Carlson

Ghosts of US 550   by Richard DeVore

Ghosts of Erie Canal   by Tony Gerst

Ghosts of the Ohio River   by Bruce Carlson

Ghosts of Warren County   by Various Writers

Ghosts of I-71 Louisville, KY to Cleveland,OH   by Bruce Carlson

Ghosts of Ohio's Lake Erie shores & Islands Vacationland by B. Carlson

Ghosts of Des Moines County   by Bruce Carlson

Ghosts of the Wabash River   by Bruce Carlson

Ghosts of Michigan's US 127   by Bruce Carlson

GHOSTS OF I-79   **BY BRUCE CARLSON**

Ghosts of US-66 from Ft. Smith to Flagstaff   by Connie Wilson

Ghosts of US 6 in Pennslyvania   by Bruce Carlson

Ghosts of the Missouri River   by Marcia Schwartz

Ghosts of the Tennessee River in Tennessee   by Bruce Carlson

Ghosts of the Tennessee River in Alabama

Ghosts of Michigan's US 12 by R. Rademacher & B. Carlson

Ghosts of the Upper Savannah River from Augusta to Lake Hartwell by Bruce Carlson

Mysteries of the Lake of the Ozarks   Hean & Sugar Hardin

GHOSTS OF CALIFORNIA'S STATE HIGHWAY 49   BY MOLLY TOWNSEND

Ghosts of La Salle County   by Joan Kalbacken

Ghosts of Illinois River by Sylvia Shults

Ghosts of lincoln Highway in ohio   By Bruce Carlson

Ghosts of the Susquehanna river   By Bruce Carlson

Ghostly Tales of Route 66: AZ to CA   by Connie Corcoran Wilson

Ghosts of the Natchez Trace   by Larry Hillhouse

To Order Copies

Please send me _____ copies of *Ghosts of the Missouri River* at $9.95 each plus $3.50 S/H. (Make checks payable to **QUIXOTE PRESS.**)

Name _____

Street _____

City _____State _____ Zip _____

QUIXOTE PRESS
3544 Blakslee Street
Wever, IA 52658
1-800-571-2665

- - - - - - To Order Copies - - - - - -

Please send me _____ copies of *Ghosts of the Missouri River* at $9.95 each plus $3.50 S/H. (Make checks payable to **QUIXOTE PRESS.**)

Name _____

Street _____

City _____State _____ Zip _____

QUIXOTE PRESS
3544 Blakslee Street
Wever, IA 52658
1-800-571-2665